Tales of the Paranormal

A collection of short stories

By

S.M. Nevermore

Content copyright S.M. Nevermore 2019. All rights reserved.

No part of this book may be reproduced in any form or by any electronic or mechanical means including information storage and retrieval systems, without permission in writing from the author. The only exception is by a reviewer, who may quote short excerpts in a review.

This book is a work of fiction. Names, characters, places, and incidents either are products of the author's imagination or are used fictitiously. Any resemblance to actual persons, living or dead, events, or locales is entirely coincidental.

- v2 –

Paperback version ISBN-13: 978-1079160581

Table of Contents

Introduction 1
A Demon's Game 5
A Familiar's Guidance 17
Haunting at Spider Gate Cemetery 33
The Yule Tree 51
So, You Finally Died! 69
Masquerade 81
Keepers of the Crystals - January: Garnet 95
A Villainous Comeback: Envy 123
The Kept Wolf 155
The Sapphire Named Ruby 179
About the Author 197

Introduction

Welcome to my world. My fictional world, that is. The stories you are about to read delve into the strange, unusual, and intriguing world of the paranormal. The paranormal fictions, romance, and fantasy in this collection contain creatures near and dear to my heart. Demons, Witches, familiars, ghosts, and more grace these pages and give you glimpses into their lives; so to speak. I took great pleasure in bringing these characters to life and I sincerely hope you enjoy them as much as I do.

Blessed Be.

A DEMON'S GAME

A MALICIOUSLY WICKED
SHORT STORY

1

IN THE
DEMON SUMMONING SERIES

S.M. NEVERMORE

A Demon's Game

Dust scattered over her piece of paper, smudging the ink from her pen. Grimacing, she crumpled the page and chucked it into the trash.

She grabbed another sheet of paper. "Do you mind? I'm trying to work."

"But I'm bored!" a voice above her whined. "Can't you at least work on something interesting, Celeste?"

When she ignored him he pouted, flipped upside down, and drifted lower until he was an inch away from her face.

"Celeeeeeeste," he whined.

"Urgh!" She threw down her pen and dragged her fingers through her black hair. "Of all the spirits in this world, and the next, I had to end up with a demon with ADD."

"Huh?"

"Attention Deficit Disorder. You have the attention span of a gnat."

"Well if you did something besides star charts and making smudge sticks it might hold my attention for more than two seconds."

Celeste sat back and scowled at the demon.

It was a rite of passage for a Witch, once she reached twenty-one, to summon a spirit. But once a spirit is released there is no controlling it. Most spirits only stay for an hour or so. She, somehow, managed to summon a demon who wanted nothing more than to stick around and pester her. And, the best part, only she could see him.

He was tall, for a demon, and if he chose to stand on solid ground he would hit about five-foot-eight. His shoulder length shaggy hair was black and his silver eyes always sparkled with mischief. He favored dressing as a harlequin joker, minus the hat, patterned in large black and white diamonds.

"Fine, what do you want to do?"

"I'm up for anything," he said and continued to float about the room, still upside down.

"How about the park?"

"No."

"The library?"

"No."

"The craft store?"

"No."

"Zane!" She threw the pen at him and missed by an inch.

"Suggest something interesting and I'll say yes."

"Look, I'm going out to get some ingredients. Come if you want; I don't care either way." She pushed herself from her chair, crossed the room to grab her purse, and headed for the door.

As she locked up her apartment, Zane passed through the wall and joined her.

She cast him a warning glare which he ignored as he started ahead of her down the sidewalk.

This was the most difficult part of having a demon around; she had to walk as if there wasn't anyone else around. If she started talking to him it would seem as if she were talking to herself and everyone would think she was crazy. It was bad enough she was one of the few Witches in town and that alone made some people nervous; she didn't need to add *crazy* to her resume.

She bit her tongue and forced herself to ignore Zane as he started causing trouble.

A fruit vendor's watermelons suddenly scattered across the sidewalk as a leg of his cart broke off. A woman's skirt flew up over her head, eliciting a scream, despite there being nothing but a gentle breeze. Dogs began rabid barking at nothing, scaring a few young children nearby and causing them to cry.

If this kept up she would be Witch, crazy, and bad luck all rolled into one. She knew these things only happened when she walked by. She would have to ask Zane to cause trouble far away from her when they went somewhere.

Zane was more of a trickster than anything else. However, she had seen what he could really do when he was angry - car accidents, broken elevators, glass shattering, objects falling; all kinds of mayhem. She had seen people seriously injured because of him and he would laugh it off.

Luckily, today didn't seem to be one of those days. Today he only wanted to cause minor problems in people's lives.

She had to ignore it all as she continued down to the local apothecary shop and quickly slipped inside. There was a small sign on the counter that read "Performing a Reading, Please Await Service," and in small text, "video surveillance in use."

Celeste shook her head and went about inspecting crystals and charms. It only took a few more minutes for Zane to find her and smile triumphantly. But her lack of enthusiasm for what he did didn't seem to diminish his mood in the least. In fact, he ignored her and began looking around for himself at what was in the store.

"Now, Mrs. Leeman, the cards aren't one hundred percent. Things can change by will and by accident."

Celeste turned.

A tall woman with chocolate brown skin emerged from a beaded curtain in the corner of the room; with her was a middle aged woman tightly clutching her purse.

"I-I know..." The woman stammered, "I just needed some proof. Thank you." The woman paid for her reading and quickly left the shop.

Celeste asked as she headed for the counter, "What did Mrs. Leeman want today, Jane?"

Jane opened the cash register and inserted the money.

"Same thing as always - a tarot reading to find out if her husband is cheating on her," she said casually, toying with a lock of her long curly hair, held back by a purple headband.

Celeste would die for those curls.

Today Jane had chosen an amethyst purple cotton dress and a shimmering silver eye shadow to match.

Celeste asked, "Is he?"

"Of course he is - the cards tell me so. But she's looking for any excuse to cling to her marriage." She laughed and folded her arms on the counter.

In addition to giving readings, Jane was a licensed pharmacologist and grew medicinal plants in an organic green room. She sold her natural treatments and medications which she made in the back of the shop. She produced everything from headache cures to ointments and creams. Her allergy medicine flew off the shelves come spring and her cold remedies come fall.

She was also Celeste's best friend.

"So," Jane set her elbows on the counter, steepled her hands together and rested her chin on them. "What can I do for you?"

"Besides, *someone* being bored, I need some ingredients. Dry are fine but fresh if you have any."

"Ah," Jane's voice suddenly hushed as if it were a secret. "So he's still around?"

Zane cried in indignation, "I'm right here!"

He flew directly in front of Jane but she could not see. Celeste pretended to see through him.

"Yes, yes he is," she sighed. "Dry ingredients are fine, live if you have them," she repeated by way of changing the subject.

"Come on in back."

Jane led the way through the back of the store and out to the back yard of the property. Her green room was almost farm sized to accommodate the merchandise she grew. Plants were in bloom in every corner and everything was categorized by the type, the use, and then alphabetized.

"You have way too much time on your hands," Celeste teased as she made her way between the rows and rows of pots.

Zane examined the plants, staying well away from some of them.

"You know..." Jane once more chose to whisper to Celeste as they walked. "We could always banish him. It would be fairly simple to do. I mean, you summoned him three months ago - he should be long gone by now."

Zane growled and popped up in front of them. "I can hear you."

Celeste could see that Jane was working on his last nerve. She did not want him harming her or the store. Some of these plants were irreplaceable.

"Really, Jane, it's fine. I appreciate the offer but I'm fine."

"Celeste, you can't want a demon around. Any spell you make will turn sour and end up being a curse."

Zane's eyes began to glow a fiery red. His growl deepened in his throat, "Tell her to shut up."

"Jane, seriously, it's okay."

She watched Zane's face as it took on a blue tinge, darkening to near black, while his eyes got even redder. She maybe had one more chance to stop the disaster before it got started. "He's not too much trouble. I actually enjoy having someone around to talk to. It gets kind of lonely in that apartment. My neighbors think I talk to myself but I can deal with that. It's nothing new when you think about it."

Jane was insistent. "Celeste, listen to yourself. You're in the company of a demon and you're okay with it. Your aura is starting to turn black because of him. You need exorcise him now before it's too late."

Celeste knew Jane meant well but she could feel the energy in the room shifting, darkening.

Jane continued, "If you don't get rid of him, the coven will and it won't be painless for either of you."

Zane roared, "Enough!"

Pots shattered, scattering plants and dirt in every direction. Wind howled in a cyclone and debris lashed at them like daggers on all sides.

Celeste's cries were drowned by the noise. "Zane, stop!"

If she didn't stop this now he could kill them both and level the store with little effort on his part.

She scrambled to try and rhyme words in her head before screaming into the storm. She chanted as loudly as she could-

"Anger that swarms and turns,
Rage that swells and burns.
Take it now, take it away,
Bring calm for at least a day.
Take this spell, take this tempest,
Do what's right, do what's best.
Calm this demon, let him rest."

The cyclone whipped the spell into the air.

Zane's intense rage countered the spell.

The wind tore into their clothes and skin like razor blades.

Jane screamed as shards of pottery lacerated her face and hands. She was forced to cover her face with her hands to protect her eyes from being damaged but could do nothing to shield the rest of her body. Her clothes were torn and blood dripped from her shallow wounds.

Before Celeste could reach for her, arms circled her waist and pulled her back.

The deep enraged voice spoke through the thunder of the wind. "You humans think you can tell me what to do?"

Jane uncovered her face only because the voice had startled her. Her eyes widened in horror and she staggered back, tripping over a fallen pot and onto the floor but still she continued to gape.

Celeste looked up at Zane and cringed, now knowing what had frightened Jane so.

Zane had allowed himself to be seen.

His skin was dark blue and his eyes were pools of lava. What had once been a joker was now a black cloak wearing, skeletal wing flapping, demon with claws that dug into her flesh.

She had only ever seen him this way once, the very first night she had summoned him into this world. The very same night that he had refused to leave.

He seethed, "I refuse to let any of you exorcise me."

She begged, "Zane, stop!"

He ignored Celeste and stared daggers at Jane.

Jane shook.

Celeste tried to free herself again.

His grip tightened and his claws punctured her skin.

Rivers of blood stained her clothes.

"She's mine to do with as I please just as is the world she released me into. Remember that, human."

Celeste's eyes widened.

Before she could try again to cast a spell, he snapped his fingers.

She was back in her apartment.

Her hair was a wind torn mess. Her clothes were shredded in places and blood soaked her sleeves from his claws. Her face was bruised and sliced and somewhere along the way she'd lost a shoe and her purse.

Zane had resumed his everyday guise. No longer was his skin a death's blue; his wings and cloak had vanished leaving him in his black and white checkered joker ensemble.

He'd released her and was floating as if reclining on a sofa, his head propped up on his hand and examining his checkered painted nails for scratches.

She screeched, "What the hell was that?"

"I was proving a point," he said as he looked up from his hand.

"And that point was?"

He shrugged. "That I'm not going anywhere, ever."

"You could've killed us!"

Amusement danced in his eyes and mirrored his smirk. "What should we do tomorrow?"

* * *

Books 2 & 3 in this series are available now.

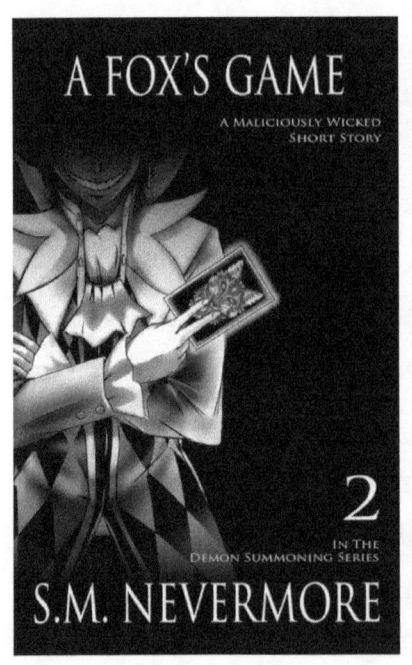

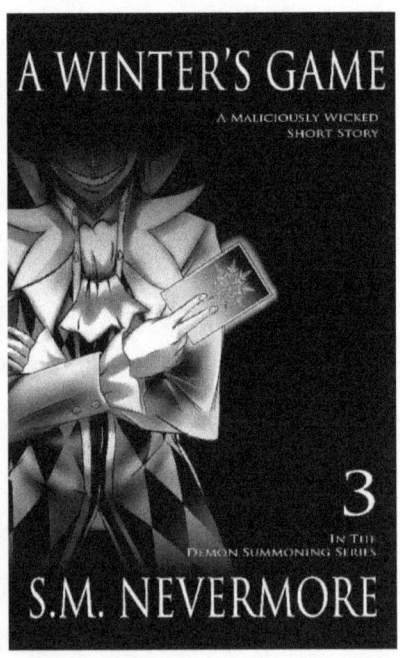

A Familiar's Guidance

Of all days to get caught...

S. M. NEVERMORE

A Familiar's Guidance

A dense silver cloud of smoke puffed into the air, causing her a harsh fit of coughs. She waved her hand to clear the smoke but it only became thicker, blinding her to the point she couldn't even see her hands in front of her face. Adding Cherry Blossom seeds had caused the chimney-like effect. What few seeds remained she slipped into her pocket.

A condescending voice came through the smoke, "I told you not to add that ingredient."

"The book told me to!" she protested as she reached blindly for her desk.

"And look what happened. Maybe next time you'll listen to me when I give you sound advice."

In her mind's eye she could see him mocking her and she growled, "If you're so smart then how about you get rid of this smoke?"

He said flatly, "No hands, remember? And, besides, my magic doesn't work that way."

She muttered, "How convenient that it only works that way when you're hungry." She groped around the desk for her book. "I need to clear this smoke before-"

A deep, restrained voice came from the doorway. "Before what?"

She froze.

A gust of wind whipped her hair behind her. The smoke was pulled into a swirling, condensed, globe in the palm of the wizard's hand, cleaning up most of the mess she'd created. Irritation radiated off of him as he shot the sphere into the fire place where it exited via the chimney.

"Oh, hi, Orion." She sheepishly said and gave him a small wave. She scooted around the desk so that there would be at least one barrier between them.

The tall wizard slowly strode forward while pinching the bridge of his nose in an all too familiar way that said he was fighting to stay calm. She was used to causing that look only this time she sure she was in for far more than just a lecture.

Of all days to get caught...

The deep blue cape Orion wore had protected his black shirt and pants from the silver cloud but the cape itself now resembled a night blanketed with stars. His neatly trimmed blond hair was also liberally dusted. His green eyes blinked behind thin wire glasses only to stare her down.

She ducked her head. Her cheeks flamed red.

She hated when he gave her the *"I had to clean up your mess, again"* look. She brushed some silver out of her shoulder length black hair and watched it fall to the desk. Her own dark purple dress was covered with a similar layer of dust.

He braced his hands on the desk as he peered into the small cauldron and then at her. "Unaryn, what happened? I leave you alone for a few minutes and find my entire study invaded by shiny fog. The books, the ingredients, everything's a mess."

She kept her eyes on the desk, tracing patterns in the coating on the mahogany. "I-I was trying a new potion and it kind of... back fired."

Reaching out a hand he took the spell book and turned it to face him. "Was this the potion?"

"...Yes"

"An invisibility spell?"

"...Yes"

His eyes bugged out in fury. "That's a level seven potion- you're only a level three!" He slammed the book shut and a silver puff rose up, making her cough again. "You are cleaning every inch of this room until not one speck of dust is left. If I find even one you're doing it all over again."

"... Yes, Orion..."

A sleek black cat hopped up onto the desk and sat on the closed book.

She cocked an eyebrow at him. "How are you still clean?" The dust had gotten into every nook and cranny of the room until Orion had intervened and whisked most of it away.

The cat ignored her and stared plaintively at Orion. "I tried to warn her;" he started, "I even tried to get her to do it right but she wouldn't listen."

Unaryn gave him a pleading stare. "Hex, hush."

He swiveled his yellow-eyed gaze to her and shook his head. If he'd had hands he'd be giving her the *"shame on you"* sign while *tsking* at her.

Orion said, his voice finally returning to a normal decibel, "One of these days I'll come up with a spell so that I can understand that cat." He pulled off his glasses and conjured a cloth out of thin air to clean them.

"Believe me," she mumbled, "You're better off not knowing. I'd love a spell to block him out."

Hex stuck his tongue out at her and she returned the gesture.

Unaryn understanding animals was how she'd come to be Orion's student. She had kept her gift a secret from everyone; even her family had no idea. There was no history of magic in her family so when testers came around they skipped her house all together.

Orion rolled his eyes. "That's enough, you two." But his order went unheard.

Unaryn retracted her tongue. "I should have left you in that bush where I found you."

"Found me?" The cat scoffed. "I chose *you*, princess, not the other way around. You think it was by accident that I happened to be there, completely silent, until you wandered along?"

"Hah! That's a laugh. You meowed because I had fish in my basket on my way home. You were a skinny, ratty looking kitten. If it weren't for me you would have starved to death."

"I was not skinny or ratty. I was a svelte kitten and cute as a button too. I believe your first words to me were, "Awe, look at the kitty.""

"Yes, and if I recall your first words to me were, "You going to share that fish or just stare at me?" And if it weren't for you talking to me and complaining about how hard your life was I-"

"Would not," Orion interrupted loudly, "be my student studying the art of magic."

Unaryn's face flushed again.

Orion had been in town that day and caught her having a long debate with the kitten. Somehow, he had managed to track her down when she ran off with the kitten in her arms. When her family realized that she had the gift of magic they were eager to see her trained.

She, however, wanted nothing to do with it. Her anger had led to an unwanted magical trigger that would release her powers in disastrous ways. She'd destroyed the study three times before finally agreeing to learn; if only so she wouldn't harm anyone else.

Three years later she was still causing problems. It was a miracle she wasn't a level one, still.

"Yes," Hex agreed. "And if it weren't for Orion teaching you control I'd be one very bald cat which is *not* what I signed up for."

Before she could snap at him Orion cut her off. "Unaryn, you're a level three Witch learning elemental magic. The Masters will be here shortly to test you for next level advancement. If you fail you'll spend another year as a three. I need you to focus."

Unaryn crossed her arms over her chest and stared at the cauldron. She knew that her being promoted every year was a big deal. It reflected on her as a Witch and on Orion as a teacher. If she failed, she would put a dent in his reputation as one of the best Wizards in the realm and the rest of the community would look at her as if she weren't good enough to be his pupil.

"The cat will suffer the most if she gets demoted." Hex meowed to Orion. Despite the fact that Orion couldn't understand, he listened as if he did.

She snapped, "Hex, quiet!" and yanked the book out from under him so that he tumbled off the table. He landed smoothly on his feet and hopped back up as if nothing happened.

"It starts with a book," he whined as he paced around the desk, "but soon it'll be forgetting to put out the milk and fish, forgetting to brush me; my fur will grow too long and I'll become a matted mess. I won't be able to get a decent nap because all of my favorite spots will be used for spell working. You'll get so caught up in studying and practicing that you'll forget all about the cat!"

She growled as she viciously flipped the pages of the book, "Yeah, yeah, poor you, poor you. Woe is the cat." She found the invisibility spell again and examined it, wondering where she went wrong. "Orion, couldn't we, I don't know," she mused innocently without lifting her eyes from the pages, "reschedule the test?"

"Absolutely not," Orion said. "You've been more than ready for quite a while now. I should have had you tested months ago. You requested more time to study and I heeded it."

Hex nodded. "If you weren't so busy working on spells beyond your reach you'd be more prepared."

Unaryn's jaw tightened. "Listen you-"

Orion rolled his eyes. "Have your argument later, they'll be here-"

A loud gong sounded through the house, causing the bottles and vials to shake on the shelves and threaten to tip over.

"-now!" He turned and strode purposefully out of the room, leaving a trail of silver behind him.

Hex leapt to the ground and was hot on his heels; Unaryn had to dart around the desk and race after them to catch up.

She tracked Orion to the parlor where three women now sat in elaborate silver thrones.

Unaryn knew these women well as they were the ones who had been testing her since her official introduction to the world of magic.

The first woman, Lobelia, was a lovely blonde in her mid-twenties wearing a soft pink cape and a white dress. The second, Lilliana, was older, in her mid to late forties. She was of similar height as Lobelia but she had brown hair, wore a blue cape and an emerald dress. The last one, Lavatera, was a hunched woman with gray streaking her onyx hair. She bore a purple cape, a black dress and she clutched a tall oak wood staff in her gnarled fingers.

These three women were the High Council of Witches. They were the judges and jurors for any crime committed by any Witch or

Wizard. They were also the testers of young Witches and they had the final say in whether or not Unaryn advanced.

Lobelia asked with a soft smile, "Last minute studying?"

"Huh?" Unaryn glanced down to the book still in her hand. "Oh, n-no, just some ho-homework." She set the book down on a table.

Lilliana proclaimed, "Unaryn, you're being tested today on your mastery of elemental magic. Should you pass you will be granted level four magic."

Unaryn nodded.

Lavatera eyeballed the feline. "And, let's not have any outside help."

Hex, insulted, hopped off the sofa and, with nose and tail high in the air, sauntered out of the room.

Unaryn felt her stomach drop. "Wait!" She could see Hex's tail flick, the only part of him that hadn't rounded the doorway. "Could he stay, please? If he promises not to do any magic to help me? He's my familiar and I'd just-." Her face flushed scarlet. She peeked back at Orion, sitting on the sofa, and he gave a slight nod.

Despite how Hex and her bickered, he was still her familiar. He was there for her no matter what and he'd been her rock through the worst of times.

Hex turned around and sat in the doorway watching.

Lobelia reassured her, "It's not a crime to want comfort from a familiar in times of stress or fear."

Lavatera added, "Familiars are here to guide and help us should we need it. Today, however, we are testing *your* magic, not combined magic. He may stay as long as he agrees not to aid you during the test."

Unaryn looked to Hex and implored, "Hex, please?"

His tail swished. "You know I'm always here for you, my girl. All you need do is ask." He returned to the room and made a show of wrapping and winding around Unaryin's legs, purring loudly enough for the three guests to hear.

Unaryn bit her lip to fight off the giggles that wanted to bubble free. She desperately hoped his cheekiness wouldn't affect the women's decision to pass or fail her.

When he'd finished making a show of himself he leapt into Unaryn's arms. From there he climbed up onto her shoulders and draped himself behind her neck, his paws hanging down her front. He purred in her ear and nudged her cheek with the top of his head; his fur warmed the back of her neck.

His thoughts projected into her mind, *ready?*

As I'll ever be. Promise not to do magic?

I suppose.

Swear it, Hex.

Fine, fine. He gave her an annoyed look. *I swear on tonight's dinner and grooming that I won't do magic to help you. Happy?*

I suppose.

"Now, if we're quite finished," Lilliana hinted as she eyed Hex warningly, "this is not a structured test. You're allowed to show us any form of magic that will connect the four elements; Earth, water, fire and air. You may begin whenever you're ready."

Unaryn was on her own now. Her decisions determined whether she passed or failed, humiliating both Hex and Orion; especially Orion. She could feel her heart flutter in her chest as panic set in.

Unaryn froze.

Hex purred again and rubbed his head against her cheek. *You can do this*, he projected. *Show them what you've got, my girl.*

I don't know what to do. I-I can't move!

Unaryn, breathe, he urged.

Hex, help me.

I can't. You can do this. I know you can. Every mistake you've made has made you stronger because you needed to work harder. You have great magic within you, I know you do. Focus and show the world.

His words brought comfort but only so much.

Orion spoke but she didn't turn to look at him. "Just relax, Unaryn, you'll be fine."

Easy for him to say, he wasn't taking the test. He hadn't tested in years so how could he know she would be fine?

"O-okay…" She took a deep breath and settled herself. Her mind scrambled for some shred of an idea, some inclination as to what to show these women. If her skills weren't exceptional as a level three she would never be granted level four permission.

But what could I possible show them that they haven't seen a hundred times before from a hundred other students?

An image entered her mind in a flash and her hands moved on their own.

Hex, are you doing this?

No, this is all you. Your body knows what to do, just keep your control over your magic.

She pulled the seeds from her pocket with a cupped hand; her other hand she held over them like a protective shield.

"*Vigiln herat.*"

Power vibrated from the core of her body and flowed to the tips of her fingers. The tightness inside her unwound and her shoulders relaxed. It was like breathing in the first warm breeze of a new spring. In that first rush all sound became muted and warmth flooded through her.

This was her home.

This was her bliss.

Hex was right; she knew what to do if she just gave her magic a chance. She didn't have to fear it. She would tell it what she wanted and it would comply. Magic only wanted to play and in return it wouldn't backfire on her. If she trusted her magic, magic that came from within her, that was a part of her, then it would trust her to direct it and use it.

At her feet erupted a pile of earth deep enough to cover the seeds she then dropped.

Hex peered down with genuine interest, as he usually did with anything involving magic. Any other time, unless it involved food, he was a cat through and through.

Keep it up, he urged, tail swishing.

She smiled at the gentle praise.

"*Fost nira.*"

A gentle rain trickled from her finger tips to the soil below.

"*Nsu Hesin.*"

A marble of fire appeared in her hand. The heat was intense yet her skin did not burn. So bright was the light she'd called forth she had to close her eyes.

She offered the power of the sun to the seeds.

Hex winced and covered his eyes with his paws. *A little warning would have been nice,* he griped.

When the light faded, along with the sunspots, she stared up in awe.

Hex, when he finally opened his eyes, let out a meow of approval.

Towering over them, in full bloom, was a cherry blossom tree. The sweet fragrance tickled the senses as she breathed it in.

It was one thing to manipulate the world around you, but to bring forth life was exhausting. She'd never combined elemental magic this way; it was much harder than using one element at a time.

She was drained.

Hex nudged her. *Don't stop, Unaryn. If you stop now you'll never get going again. I can't help you. You have to use your own magic.*

I can't-

Yes, you can. Center yourself. Release your magic at a steady pace. Don't release it too quickly or you'll drain yourself completely. Don't do it for me, the Masters, or even for Orion. Do this for you. You'll never forgive yourself if you give up now.

He was right, again. This was her test, her magic, and her pride on the line.

She whispered, *"Tengel zebree."*

Using the last bit of magic she could spare without hurting herself, the lightest gust of wind was pulled from her own breath and given movement through the branches.

One by one the petals were plucked from the tree, guided by the wind, to circle the Masters, and scatter their perfume about the room.

That's my girl, Hex purred.

Lobelia giggled and Liliana let out a pleased sigh, childlike delight in her eyes. The three women looked between each other as if in the midst of telepathic conversation.

Orion stood and moved beside Unaryn, putting his hand on her back to help steady her after using so much power.

"Orion," Lavatera finally began, not even the slightest bit of emotion betrayed what the final judgement might be. "You have a talented student here. Congratulations. You may begin level four training."

Unaryn let out a relieved laugh. She reached up and rubbed her eyes to hide the stray tears that wanted to leak free. When she opened them again the women were gone, chairs and all.

Orion smiled. "You did well, Unaryn, I'm very proud."

Hex stood up on her shoulders. "I am too. Very nice, little Witch. Now, how about we go feed the cat?" He hopped down and looked up at the large tree. "After you remove this from the parlor."

Unaryn blinked up at the tree in total loss. She had brought about this tree but she had no idea how to remove it.

She bit her lip and giggled.

She turned her eyes up to Orion and smiled innocently. "So, does that mean I can try that invisibility spell now?"

HAUNTING AT SPIDER GATE CEMETERY

*if you toy with spirits they'll toy with you.
They don't all play nice.*

S. M. NEVERMORE

Haunting at Spider Gate Cemetery

I told myself that we should have stayed at the party. There was no need for us to be out here.

I announced, "This is a bad idea," as we traipsed through the cemetery.

The old stones set in neat rows were rough but well cared for. Most of the names could still be read clearly. During the day I was sure that the cemetery was lovely. However, the night changed things.

Tara laughed. "This is a must on Halloween. Where's your sense of adventure? Where's your curiosity?"

Lindsay, bringing up the rear, laughed with her. "Don't be such a baby, Amy. This is right up your alley. I thought you'd be ecstatic when we told you where we were going."

Okay, I may be a Goth and I may dress tough, but I know the difference between a good idea and an incredibly foolish one. I know that you never toyed with spirits.

Spirits were unpredictable and potentially dangerous. There was no controlling them. And they don't take well to teasing or tormenting. They could be passive and not care at all about being called, if done respectfully, or they could be destructive. Even when you were respectful in every sense, sometimes the spirit itself was innately wicked and would cause problems. It was risky business that was not worth getting into.

I'd never called on spirits before.

Sure, I knew how. But I had never done so or even seen it done.

My mentor had warned me against it many times. She'd cautioned me that I wasn't ready or prepared to handle the responsibility of dealing with the spirit world.

I agreed with her now more than ever.

I also knew it was a foolish idea to be traipsing through Quaker Cemetery, A.K.A. Spider Gates cemetery, but I had been powerless to deter my friends. However if I didn't go with them they would do something even more disastrous than calling a spirit or two. I had spent the entire ride to Leicester trying to talk some sense into them to no avail.

I even tried to buy time by causing a traffic jam halfway to Leicester. It had cost quite a bit of magic but I had been desperate.

I cursed myself for not bringing salt or Moon-blessed holy water to purify the ground my friends chose. This was not hallowed ground; years of superstitions and negative energies had blackened the land.

There was a reason this cemetery was closed at night.

Supposedly a boy had hung himself in the cemetery and where he did so there now lay a patch of ground where grass no longer grew. Another rumor was that a girl was said to have been brutally murdered on the cemetery grounds. And it was said that if you go through each of the eight gates of the cemetery you'll enter the eight gates of Hell.

I gripped my pentacle necklace and prayed to the Earth, water, fire and air it represented for protection.

Something...

Something was coming.

I just couldn't tell *what*.

I wanted to turn tail and run back home where it was safe and warm.

Trees became clawed creatures of the night and moaned in agony as the wind rustled their branches. A dense fog crawled between the trees like fingers itching to snatch whatever they could reach. The tomb glowed under the light of a full moon and disfigured shadows floated unattached over hills and crevices.

Nightmares suddenly seemed all too real as that familiar chill made its way up my spine, making my hair stand on end and my body quiver. Even my heart felt the change in the air; it beat like a drum in my ears.

When we reached the raised part of the cemetery, also known as "The Altar," we set out the candles and the Ouija board. This was the part of the cemetery that was raised only a few inches high but spanned about twenty feet with trees surrounding it. We arranged the candles in a circle around where we would be sitting and the Ouija board was placed in the center.

Tara, dressed as a gypsy, sat down by the board and waited for us to join her.

Lindsay, dressed as a cow girl, got to work lighting the candles. It was a struggle with the wind factor but when the wind died down she was able to light them all. She sat down with us and slid the lighter into her boot.

Tara asked, evil smirk playing on her lips, "Ready?"

I tried to protest again. "It's a bad idea. I told you, you don't want to anger the spirits, especially on Halloween. Something terrible always happens when you do."

"We're not going to make anyone angry. Would you stop worrying? Besides I've done this before and I've never even gotten so much as a twitch from the board."

Lindsay secured the tie for her hat under her chin. "I don't even believe in ghosts. I just do this for fun."

I muttered, "Real fun..."

Tara motioned for the three of us to put our hands on the pointer. Lindsay and I had two hands on the dial while Tara only had one; her other hand held a pen and a pad of paper on her knee.

When she caught me looking she said, "Just in case we get something. You never know." She cleared her throat and closed her eyes. "Oh spirits of Halloween," she began in a lilting voice. "We beseech you. Show yourself. Make your presence known to us."

She and Lindsay broke into a fit of giggles.

It felt as if something were crawling up my spine, making me shudder and shift uncomfortably. Neither of them seemed to notice.

If I started freaking out they either wouldn't believe me or would run screaming in the wrong direction. In this darkness someone would fall and break a leg.

When the feeling passed I calmed.

They finally got their laughter under control and Tara cleared her throat again. "Oh spirits come to us on this night, All Hallows Eve, when the barrier between our world and the spirit world is at its thinnest."

Lindsay was biting her lip to keep another fit of giggles from surfacing.

Tara waited a few minutes before she sighed in defeat. "I give up. Lindsay, you try."

"Fine, fine," she said and straightened up.

That feeling was coming back.

Only this time it was worse, painful.

Claws raked down my back and it took everything I had not to scream.

"Guys," I fought the whimper in my voice. "Seriously, we should stop. Spirits don't like to be played with. They're not toys for us to use and throw away when we get bored. We should stop now and go back to the party."

"Oh, don't be such a baby," Lindsay said. "Nothing's going to happen. It was dull anyway. Not even a good game of truth or dare could wake that party up. We might as well have been in a cemetery already. So this isn't much of a scenery change. Come on, it's your turn."

"I want no part of this."

"Then why are you here?"

"To try and talk some sense into you two. We're going to get hurt if we keep this up."

Tara sighed heavily. "If I knew you were going to be this much of a party pooper I never would have invited you."

I ignored the sting of her words. "Please, can we go?"

"No. It took us forever to get here from Grafton with the traffic we hit. This place is so out of the way we circled town three times before finding it. If we get something then maybe we'll leave but with the way things are going we'll be here all night."

"But-"

"Amy, we're staying, suck it up."

They should tell that to my back. I could feel the angry scratches and knew they were a warning. I was more in tune to spirits than my friends. The creatures were threatening us, using me as an intermediary.

I could feel the eyes watching us from all corners of the cemetery.

I asked, "If you know we're not going to get anything then why are we doing this at all?"

Tara laughed, "For fun. What else?" She nodded to Lindsay.

Lindsay closed her eyes and began a mantra.

She rocked about as if in a trance, eyes fluttering and head tossed back. "Om... Om... Om... oh spirits. We call upon you now. We three seek audience with you. Make yourselves known to us. Oh Ouija, Ouija, Ouija…"

This went on for quite a while.

It was embarrassing to listen to. They had no idea the kind of bad mojo they were inviting into the circle. Now I desperately wished

I had brought my supplies for protection. I might be able to stave off the inevitable.

I continued to refuse to make calls so the two of them passed the task back and forth until finally Tara was more than frustrated with the whole thing. She threw down her pen and glared at the night sky, the full moon high and bright overhead.

I shifted as a fresh gust moaned through the trees. "Tara," I warned, "Stay calm. Don't get carried away and do something you'll regret."

She shouted into the air, "All right, I demand you show yourselves. Now."

Lindsay winced. "Too late."

"You heard me! Come out!"

The world went still.

A dead silence so enveloping it made my ears pop.

Lindsay had gone pale and Tara's wide eyes darted about.

Maybe the spirits had left. Maybe they'd tired of this game and decided that the three of us weren't worth it.

"Come on, guys. Let's go-"

The wind whipped up in an angry cyclone so intense it forced me flat to the ground.

The candles went dark in an instant and plunged us back into a world of nightmares.

We screamed.

I didn't notice the wind had stopped until I realized we were the only ones making noise.

It's over. It has to be.

I pushed myself up. I could see nothing but I could hear the pained and frightened whimpers of my friends not far from me.

It was too quiet.

No leaves rustling, no animals scurrying about, not even the gentlest breeze stirred.

Something wicked this way comes; and with a vengeance.

Tara cussed, "Damn it. Lindsay, do you still have the lighter?"

I heard a rustling beside me as Lindsay went into her boot for her lighter.

Click.

A lonely little flame jumped to life.

I was finished with all of this. We were leaving even if I had to drag them back one at a time.

I reached out to pick up the Ouija board pointer.

It moved.

I jerked my hand back.

Lindsay and Tara stared at the board, transfixed, as the dial slithered on its own.

I grabbed the discarded pen and paper and began writing down every letter the dial hovered over.

I read out loud as I wrote. "You... wanted... us... well... here... we... are..."

I looked up at my friends but they had gone pale.

Lindsay was shaking.

The moon darkened behind a cloud.

Shadows converged on us like an army and walled us within the circle of candles.

The flickering flames were the only things keeping the spirits at bay.

I watched in horror as the darkness surged forward and claimed the flames like a starving beast.

Then I heard it.

A laugh.

A child's laugh.

A little girl's laugh.

It chilled me to my core and made my heart clench.

It began to sing, *"Ring around the rosy-"*

I slowly stood, still holding the pen and paper. "Girls," I whispered, "When that last candle goes out-"

Five to go.

"A pocket full of posies-"

"We run."

Three.

"Ashes, ashes-"

"Don't stop till you reach the gate."

"We all fall-"

Two.

"Don't look back."

One.

Darkness.

"DOWN!"

"GO!"

We ran.

We leapt over rocks, roots and rounded tombstones.

The wind picked up its howl, whipping and tearing at our hair and clothes. It angrily circled us and tried in vain to force us back to the Altar.

Tara broke free first and raced ahead of us. A hand covered in rot and ripped flesh darted out from between the tomb stones and grabbed her ankle.

She screamed and crashed to the ground. Blood gushed from her nose and her hands clawed at the dirt in a desperate attempt at escape.

Another hand reached out to grip her other ankle and yanked her back.

No longer was there a cemetery behind us. Instead there was darkness so complete that no candle could ever hope to penetrate. And Tara was being dragged into it against her will.

Her scream was blood curdling.

I was too far away to make it in time but Lindsay dove for Tara and snatched her wrists.

Tara sobbed, "Don't let go! Don't let go!"

Lindsay was struggling to pull Tara free. "Amy! Help!"

I raced forward to grab hold but the dead hands yanked harder and wrenched Tara from Lindsay's saving grasp.

"HEEEEELP!"

"Tara!" Lindsay scrambled to her feet.

I ran between the stones to follow but the disembodied giggling started again and I halted.

She was close.

I shouted into the darkness, "Give her back!"

She sang, *"Three blind mice, three blind mice-"*

She was singing about us.

"Stop it!"

"See how they run, see how they run."

"She's not yours!"

"They all ran after the farmer's wife, who cut off their tails with a carving knife-"

"I'm not running from you."

"Did you ever see such a sight in your life, as three blind mice?"

The voice went silent.

Lindsay and I scanned the darkness but I saw them first.

I screamed, "Run!"

I shoved her in front of me and raced towards the gates. The body-less hands sprinted after us, using the ground to propel themselves forward.

Lindsay caught her foot on a tree root and fell. "OW!" She clutched her wrist and pulled it protectively to her chest. "Amy, help Me-mnph!"

Two hands seized at her hair and covered her mouth to keep her from screaming. Her eyes shrieked of unbridled terror. She thrashed furiously and I clawed at the hands to wrench her free.

Two more rotted hands joined the fray and dug into Lindsay's ankles.

One leapt at me.

I ducked in time to receive only a shallow scratch on my cheek that had been intended for my eyes.

But it had been enough of a distraction.

Lindsay screamed as the hands grabbing her hair and arms yanked her back into the darkness.

I charged after her.

Her screams abruptly cut off; another, familiar, voice took her place.

"Mary, Mary, quite contrary, how does your garden grow?"

"Let them go! Please, let them go!"

"With silver bells, and cockle shells, and pretty maids all in a row."

She was coming after me next.

I ran.

I ran for my life.

Tears dripped down my face.

The moon unveiled itself and I could see the gates ahead of me.

Strength I didn't even know I had surfaced in my desperation to escape.

I crashed through the metal gates so hard they rang with a *gong* against the stone wall before shutting.

I fell to my knees and struggled to settle my heart.

The tears I had begun to shed fell onto my hands.

I turned to look behind me.

The world was calm.

A gentle breeze rustled the trees and scattered the leaves on the ground. I could hear an owl hooting. All was as it should be.

I had been powerless to save my friends.

I'd known that something was going to happen. The warning signs had been there but I hadn't been able to do a damn thing to help them.

I was useless.

My tears blurred my vision and the pressure in my chest begged for release. I turned my face to the moon and released the hurt and pain I felt deep within. I screamed until shards of glass shredded my throat with every wail. I screamed until I'd emptied my heart.

When I could scream no more I dissolved into quiet sobs.

A gentle voice spoke behind me, "Amy."

I sniffed, straightened, and wiped my tears. "I know. Don't say it."

"You warned them."

I shouted through my tears, "I know!"

"Don't blame yourself for this."

My shoulders slumped as I struggled to keep my composure. "They can't be gone. They can't!"

I turned.

Behind me stood a tall, lovely woman in her early sixties. She had long silver hair and softly wrinkled skin. It made her look wise rather than aged. She wore a long purple cloak with the hood pushed back.

I begged her, "Tell me what to do. Please, I'll do whatever it takes."

She gently turned me around so she could lift the back of my shirt to see the bloody scratches. I winced as I felt the sting of her healing them. As soon as she was done I turned again to face her.

"Nora, please!" I could feel tears threaten again.

Her eyes betrayed how little there was we could do. "Amy…"

I implored, "But it was her."

Morgana's eyes furrowed. "Who, her?"

"The girl, the one that was murdered here. She-she was laughing and singing. She blew out the candles like a birthday cake. She was the one who sent those demons after us."

Morgana glanced away.

I knew that look.

Morgana was going through every spell she knew to try and fit spell to scenario. Running rituals, group circles, and moon phases through her mind all at once. It was as if she were seeing the future and just how each spell would result.

"Morgana?"

She shook her head. "No."

My face fell. "What? Why?"

"We don't tamper with the spirit world. You warned your friends and they chose to ignore you. Be grateful you were not taken as well."

"I... I didn't anger them."

"Which is why you only received a warning. Next time they won't be so lenient. It's best we leave this place lest the spirits change their minds."

"But-"

"Your friends are lost to us. There's nothing to be done." Morgana put an arm around my shoulders and started walking me away from the cursed grounds. "Come along."

I glanced back at the gates, tears streaking my cheeks.

I whispered in defeat, "I warned you."

The Yule Tree

*The Yule Spirit
Comes But
Once A Year*

S. M. NEVERMORE

The Yule Tree

What is a Yule tree? The Yule tree is a pagan tradition going back centuries. Originally, trees were brought into the home to keep wood spirits warm during the long, cold winter months. Food and goodies were hung on the branches as offerings to these wood spirits. Bells were hung in addition so that they might chime when an appreciative spirit was present. A five pointed star, the pentacle, was hung atop the tree to represent Earth, Water, Fire, Air, and Spirit. The tradition was appropriated by Catholics into the traditional Christmas tree that is seen today. Whatever tree or tradition you keep in your family, may your holidays be filled with happiness, light, and love.

The voices were what woke me first. What had me shooting out of bed was the kitten at the foot of my bed trying to take a flying leap. I snatched her out of mid-air and clutched her to my chest as she squirmed for freedom.

As I listened, what I had thought was the howling winds from the winter's storm, thank you New England, was not the outside world threatening to invade the warmth of the house but small voices coming from the living room.

I swung my legs out of bed and tucked them into a pair of slippers to protect them from the hardwood floors. With kitten gnawing on my thumb, I tiptoed out of my room and peeked around the corner.

Two bright lights zipped around the darkened tree in a frenzy. The cat caught sight and tried to frantically get free. I held firm and watched.

The blue light asked in a high voice that made me smile. "Are you sure this is the right tree?"

"Right tree? It's the only tree!" came the pink light that flew to the top where the pentacle tree topper sat. "Every other tree on the block is a Christmas tree. This is the first, and only, Yule tree we could find in an emergency. It's not my fault the tradition was plagiarized by others."

"Yes, but will it work?"

"We don't know until we try."

The blue light hovered near the center of the tree and I now noticed a faint green light among the branches. However, it was only a flicker among the shadows.

"Even if it's not a Yule tree," the blue one continued, "it's the best we can do."

The pink one huffed, "If it's not a Yule tree it won't work. Intent is everything."

"Well," the blue one darted down, almost colliding with the pink one, "how do you know it's *not* a Yule tree?"

"We don't know that it is and we don't know that it isn't."

"Look at it!" The pink one started making rounds about the tree. "Painted pine cone ornaments, strung acorns, painted sigils, pentacle on top; this is clearly a Yule tree."

"But it's a fake tree! How is it supposed to work if the tree is a fake? At least some of the other trees were real- a little dry- but real."

"Like you said, intent is everything. Maybe it will still work even though it's not a real tree. Everything about this tree screams Yule. Although, I don't quite get the Samhain decorations. I think this Witch is a little bit confused about what time of year it is." She paused. "Maybe we *should* find a new tree."

I came around the corner and flicked on the light switch. The two lights squeaked and vanished into the tree. Only the green one remained visible, barely.

"Samhain," I said, "is my favorite holiday. I always put my Halloween decorations on my Yule tree." I sat on the sofa and put the kitten beside me. She stared, transfixed, at the tree, but I kept her back from investigating. "You could have just asked if it was a Yule tree instead of wasting precious time speculating."

I waited patiently, but no sound came from the tree. The creatures who'd made them continued to hide from me.

"You know," I said, "if you told me what was wrong I might be able to help. The way you two were talking it seemed like time was of the essence."

There was another prolonged period of silence but if I listened hard enough I could faintly hear a heated whispering debate going on.

I gasped, "Mikari! Bad girl! Don't climb the tree!"

"CAT!"

They shot out of the tree like bullets and I covered my mouth to keep from laughing. The cat tried to jump off the couch but I continued to hold her back.

When the faeries saw the cat was not, in fact, hunting them down the blue one glared. "Mean!"

"I'm sorry," I smiled, "how else was I going to get you two to come out?" I put the kitten down on the floor where she watched the two faeries intently.

I held my hands out and flat.

They hesitated but my patience won and a faerie landed on each hand. Now that I had them close I could see past their glow to their features.

Both faeries were about five inches tall. The pink fairy was pale with soft brown hair done in a loose braid with the tail pulled forward over her shoulder. Her dress was deep pink and looked to be made of flower petals. The skirt was made of individual petals that reached her knees and the sleeveless bodice was made of petals that had been woven together. Her wings were almost translucent and so soft a pink that it seemed spun sugar had been used to make them.

The blue fairy was dark skinned. Her deep brown hair was streaked with mahogany and pulled up into a high tail; tight ringlets fell down her back. Her dress was also the same color as her glow. The halter-style dress looked to be fashioned from snowflakes that had been knitted together. The webbings of the dress fashioned a lace-style top of an icy shade that gradually deepened to a dark blue at the skirt which flowed around her ankles. Her wings were a similar color to her dress and faded from dark blue at her back to icy white at the tips and sparkled like fallen snow.

I felt very frumpy in my bed head and sushi pajamas.

"Now," I said as the two fairies settled into my hands, "what is so important that you two had to sneak into my home in the middle of the night during a blizzard?"

The two creatures looked at each other, the pink one biting at her nails and the blue one twirling her hair.

"Okay," I decided, "let's try again. What are your names?"

The blue one answered first, "I'm Evergreen."

"I'm Holly," answered the pink one.

I smiled. "I'm Jolene. It's lovely to meet you both. I've never met fairies before."

Holly smiled back. "We've never met a Witch before. Although, we do see humans, Witches and animals all the time, we just don't interact with them."

"Oh? Why not?"

"Well, we want to. It's just that-"

"People don't see us," Evergreen finished. "Animals see us, Witches are open to us but it's hard to interact with other humans around. Children see us most of the time since their eyes aren't clouded and their minds are open. But, most don't see us so we can't interact."

I knew that with trees and land being cleared all the time it was harder for creatures to keep homes and their powers. It was a sad fact of life for these amazing creatures and I was powerless to help them on the grand scale. But, I could do something right now.

"I can see you, which either means I'm very open or you needed to be seen. Either way, I can help if you'll let me."

The fairies glanced at each other again. I could almost see the silent communication between them as they wrestled with what to do.

I gave them the time they needed. Obviously what they had brought with them was of grave importance or they wouldn't have risked entering a human dwelling. If the little light in the tree was any indication of what it was then it could be a matter of life or death.

Holly was practically dancing on my palm and worrying her bottom lip. Evergreen was calm on the outside; her nervousness was given away by her incessant hand wringing.

"Well..." Holly started, "what happened was-"

"Mrrrow."

All three of us turned to the tree and caught a glimpse of a small black tail disappearing up the trunk of the tree.

Holly flew off my hand and plowed into the branches. "No!"

Evergreen and I watched in shock as branches shook and trembled.

"Mrrrrooow!"

"No! Shoo! Go away kitty!"

"Mrrrrr."

"Back!"

"Mew!"

The branches continued to shake and sway. I only had an idea of where they were by Holly's pink glow.

"No, no, no! Shoo!"

I stood and Evergreen fluttered from my hand. I hurried to the tree and reached into the branches. When my hand found her scruff I carefully extricated Mikari. She mewed in protest but I put her on the couch where she wouldn't cause many more problems.

I reached into the tree again and gingerly lifted the green fairy. She was unconscious in my hands but she was as beautiful as her companions.

Her dress was made of grass with the blades forming a loose skirt. The bodice was off shoulder with three quarter sleeves also made out of intricately woven grass pieces. Her skin was softly sun kissed. Her acorn colored hair was liberally streaked with blonde and hung loose around her shoulders.

I could already see problems on the surface besides her unconscious state. Various cuts and bruises marred her arms and legs; a nasty bruise was on her cheek and forehead. If I hadn't seen the slight rise and fall of her chest I would have panicked that she was dead. Her glow was too faint for my liking and she was cold despite having been in the house for long enough to have started warming up.

I sat down on the couch, keeping the fae well away from the curious nose of my kitten.

Gingerly I bent her legs and arms to see if anything caused her pain enough to wake up or even stir.

"No!" Holly flew to my face and spread her arms out as if to block my view, or access, to the prone fairy in my hands. "You'll hurt her!"

I smiled sympathetically but was firm when I said, "I know you're worried and I know that she is the reason you two risked coming in here. If I don't try to help her she might not make it."

Evergreen came forward and gently pulled Holly back. She asked, "Please help her. We don't know how. It would have taken too long to get her to a healer fairy and she was so cold."

I looked back down at the fairy. "How did this happen?"

Evergreen guided Holly to sit on the arm of the sofa and settled beside her.

Evergreen explained, "We were out making sure all was well. I'm a winter fairy and I'm responsible for making sure no two snowflakes are alike. Holly is a flower fairy. She's responsible, at this time of year, for making sure all plants are hibernating. Sometimes a few plants hang on longer than they should and she needs to make sure they sleep. Ivy is an animal fairy. She has to go around and make sure that all of the animals which are supposed sleeping for the winter are, in fact, sleeping." She looked to Ivy mournfully. "We found her in the snow."

Holly added, "We were making our last rounds for the night. Your backyard and the two beside you are our jurisdiction, so to speak. Every night we go out with several other fairies and work. We finish shortly before dawn on most nights and we meet up at the tree stump in your neighbors' back yard." Holly choked on her words but she kept going, "We waited an hour for Ivy. The other three went back to the grove to warn the queen that something might have gone wrong. Evergreen and I went to try to find Ivy. And, we did, hanging off a branch."

Tears dripped from Holly's eyes and Evergreen hugged her tightly.

If I had to guess what had happened I would have put my money on an animal that wasn't sleeping, but should have been, was up and about and hungry. One caught the other by surprise and the fairy was attacked. She was lucky to be alive at all. It was below freezing outside and despite their ability to survive in any natural environment, being unconscious in the snow was a sure fire way to die.

I couldn't promise that she wasn't going to die or that I could make her recover. Still, I knew I could try and do my best by her. "Let's see if there's anything we can do to speed things along."

I stood from the sofa and headed for my craft room. I could hear the flutter of wings behind me along with the *click-clack* of claws on the floor. Gingerly holding the fairy in one hand, I opened the door and stood aside to let everyone else follow in. I shut the door and turned on the light.

The room was on the small side but cozy. Shelves and cabinets lined the walls, a glass curio cabinet nestled into the corner, and a low mahogany coffee table sat dead center of the room on a round plush purple rug. From the curio cabinet I withdrew a small leather notebook and two folded pieces of cloth.

The first cloth I kept folded and used as a cushion for the fairy in my hands. I set Ivy down comfortably on the table which left my hands free to do their work. I opened the second cloth and spread it out on the table. The black cloth was decorated with silver moons, stars, several pentacles, and in the center was the triple moon; two outward facing crescent moons flanking a full moon.

While the two fairies sat around their friend, the kitten watched me go about the room collecting tools, jars, and a few books from one of the shelves. For once she wasn't so intent on our guests but I knew why. She knew what I was about to do and was ready to join me. At only four months old she was already attuned to what my intentions were and how she could help me.

I sat down at the table, put out the jars and set down my athame, wand, and chalice. With everything organized I opened the two books that I relied most heavily on in my craft, my own Book of Shadows and a guide for magical herbs.

Evergreen flew over and hovered above the page I'd paused on in my Book of Shadows. She inquired warily, "What are you going to do, exactly?"

"I'm hoping to offer some protection and a little boost in her recovery. I can't cast too drastic a spell as it might do more harm than good. But, I'll do what I can."

"You won't hurt her, right?"

I could see her casting sidelong glances at the athame and I could understand her concern. "No, I won't hurt her. Neither will you."

Both fairies looked up and unified, "Me?"

"That's right. I'm going to give you two the ability to help your friend along. You, myself, and the Yule tree."

Holly, who was holding Ivy's hand, inquired, "Will it work? Evergreen had said it might not because the tree was a fake tree."

"It will work," I reassured her, "just as well as a real tree."

"Why is it a fake tree?"

"I don't believe in cutting down a tree for the purpose of keeping it for a few months and then throwing it away like it meant nothing. What was once a tradition steeped in meaning, designed to protect nature until the following spring, is now nothing more than a way to pretty up a room full of presents before getting thrown on the curb for the dumpster. Even if that was the reason for the tree being grown, I don't believe in having its life cut short."

Evergreen looked up at me. "But will it still work?"

"Neither of you need to worry; the intent is all that matters. I'll do what I can to give her a boost and then you two will give a bit of yourselves to help her."

I looked at Ivy and bit my bottom lip. Her light was growing dimmer. She was out in that cold too long after being attacked. Time was against both my magic and the fairy's light. I only prayed that we had it in us to see this to the end.

While the fairies stayed by their friend's side I got to work. I pulled a muslin drawstring bag from the shallow drawer in the table and got to work filling the bag. A pinch of lotus, eucalyptus, rosemary, and sandalwood. For good measure I added anise, wisteria, and crushed egg shell. I was about to close the bag when the kitten hopped onto the table, loudly meowed at me and nudged a rough black stone in my direction with her paw; I added the tourmaline stone without hesitation.

With the bag filled, I pulled the strings tightly to seal it securely. I opened my book again, this time turning to my chapter on sigils, special symbols drawn to invoke certain intent and desires. I found the one I had made for healing and drew it with marker onto the face of the bag.

Ivy was hanging on by a thread. If Peter Pan taught us anything, it was that when a fairy's light went out they died. Unfortunately, clapping from the audience wouldn't be enough to save this little creature.

I glanced at the clock, quickly scooped the fairy up, bag and all, and hurried back to the tree.

Evergreen and Holly raced after me. They called, "What's wrong?"

"The Witching Hour is almost over. If we don't hurry we might not make it." I situated the fairy among the branches and used the herb bag as her new bed with the sigil facing up. I turned to go back into my Craft room but stopped short when the kitten came trotting out. She carried, dragged really, in her mouth a string connected to a black pouch. I met her half way and scooped both of them up. "Good girl." She purred loudly and climbed my arm until she'd perched herself on my shoulder.

I glanced at the clock. Five minutes to four. I might not make it.

No.

She might not make it.

I opened the bag and extracted five quartz crystals. Working my way around the tree, I made quick work of setting up the stones on the floor so that they made a circle with the stones representing the five points on the pentacle.

As I did this I recited, "*I open my circle with love and light.*

Moon's glow from up above, protect those within with all your might.

Healing magic to do no harm; only good may enter here."

With my circle cast, and me back at my starting point facing the fairies, I reached into the bag and pulled out a white candle and a lighter. With a flick, I ignited the flame and lit the candle.

"Okay, girls, ready?"

The two nodded and each took hold of one of Ivy's hands then joined their own.

"When I start the spell, I want both of you to start pouring your energy into Ivy. Not too fast and not too much. I don't want either of you getting drained. When I stop, you stop."

I didn't wait for them to agree or disagree.

"*In this night and in this hour I call upon the Sacred Power.*

Healing magic be granted to we creatures three."

The two fairies began to glow brighter; their tiny eyes shut while pouring their magic into Ivy.

The kitten purred in my ear. The warm feel of her on my shoulder helped slow my racing heart.

"What I have I now share,

With my gifts I heal what was sweet and fair.

Fairy ripped from the Earth and skies,

Will now be restored so she may fly.

Lady of The Moon we ask of thee,

With your light empower we creatures three."

I held out my hand to the fairies and rested a finger atop their clenched hands. Their glow became almost white.

"In your name,

As it will be done,

So mote it be."

White hot light near blinded me and I had to shut my eyes.

"Mroooow."

I opened my eyes again and risked a darting glance at the clock. Four a.m.; the Witching Hour was over.

Please let me not be too late.

When I looked back at the fairies I saw the light was gone. In its place were Evergreen and Holly leaning anxiously over Ivy. Even the kitten was leaning out to try to see her.

Holly cried out first and leapt onto Ivy.

My heart jumped, fearing the worst when I heard her crying.

"Ivy! Thank the Goddess!"

A rushed breath left my lungs and my hand covered my heart. It was going a mile a minute.

Both Holly and Evergreen were crying. Ivy was struggling to sit up with Holly hanging onto her. I could see her confused expression.

I smiled, sat down on the sofa and put the kitten in my lap. I would give them a minute to gather themselves and enjoy their reunion.

I sighed and gently stroked Mikari's velvet fur while listening to excited chatter from the tree. A sense of peace overcame me as I realized that it was Yule morning and, for once, it wasn't a quiet one.

Blessed Be.

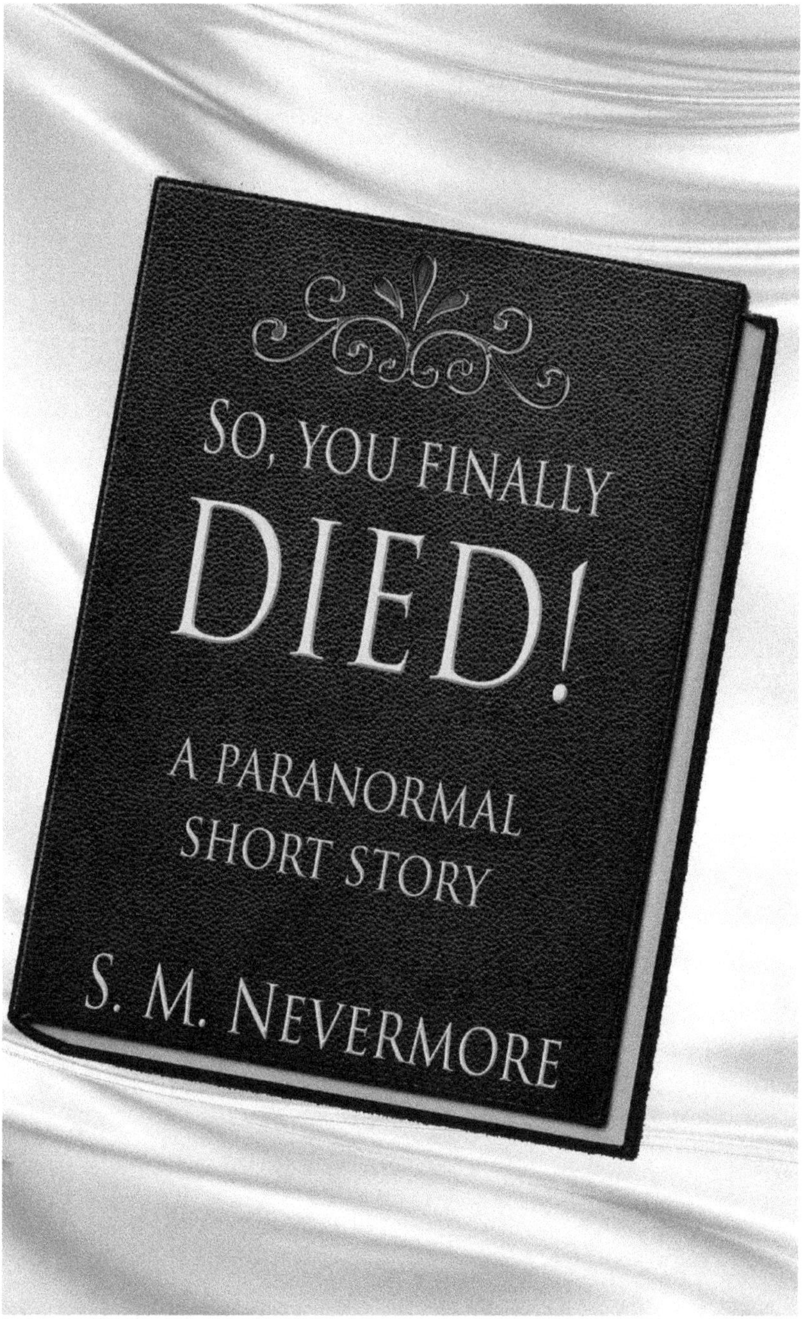
SO, YOU FINALLY
DIED!
A PARANORMAL
SHORT STORY
S. M. NEVERMORE

So, You Finally Died!

When people have near death experiences most people say they saw a bright light. Others will say they saw family and friends either waiting for them or telling them to go back, that it wasn't their time. Some have even said they saw their worst nightmares come to life in their last moments only to have them pulled back from death by the shock of the defibrillator paddles.

For me... well, that didn't happen.

One minute I was minding my own business, walking down the street, then *Boom*! I was in a windowless room with beige walls, a beige sofa and chair, a low coffee table, and a matching beige metal desk with a woman *tap, tap, tapping* away on the keyboard of her computer.

"A waiting room?" I asked in disbelief. "Really?"

"Today? Not going to happen."

I looked back at the woman. "Me?"

Still not looking up from her screen she pointed to her ear where a wireless headset rested that, I assumed, connected to the landline beside the computer. I clasped my hands behind my back and rocked on my heels while I waited.

"Uh huh," *tap, tap, tap,* "uh huh... uh huh... yeah, not today sweetie." She pressed a button on the set but continued typing.

I stood there for an unknown amount of time waiting for her to acknowledge my presence in the room. As well as their being no windows, there were no doors or clocks adorning the walls, not even a small painting to brighten the dull room.

But, in that stretch of time, I was able to get a good look at the receptionist. She wore a V-necked wide collared dress in a coral color. It had a naturally tapering waist and I would bet that the skirt was full and pleated. Her hair was blonde and cut into a bob that curled up at the ends.

If you didn't age or change when you died, as I assumed was the case since I didn't feel any younger or older, then she must've died in the fifties.

But if she died in the fifties, how does she know how to use a computer and a Bluetooth headset?

"Umm," I softly said. "Excuse me but what do I-"

A clipboard and pen were shoved under my nose in an instant. *How did she do that?*

"Fill these out and wait." One hand was still flying over the keys and her eyes never drifted.

I took the clip board and saw that there were at least ten pieces of paper under the clip and a pen chained to the board.

"But what-"

She repeated, "Fill out the forms and wait."

Now, I'm not a person who angers easily. Do I get flustered, sure. But I'm the person who keeps it in and pastes the smile on my face.

Even with the rudest customers in retail, I never let frustration it show. Parents letting their kids run amok in the store; I kindly told kids not to run. Parents on their phones who let kids tear apart toys, misplace items, or leave items where they're not supposed to go; I pick it up and keep the anger inside. A person gets mad because they can't get clearance price on an item that was left in the clearance section by another person; I kindly try to diffuse the situation. My temper was something I saved for the break room or my own home.

I was the epitome of retail kindness, grace, understanding, and reasoning; in my own humble opinion of course.

Any thoughts otherwise are just that, thoughts. I never speak my mind outright to customers or anyone else.

But this…

This was unacceptable!

I was used to being ignored in life but I wasn't going to stand for being ignored when dead.

"Look, I'll fill these out but I need to ask-"

She scoffed sarcastically, "Gee, you just bit the big one and you have questions? Big surprise!" Finally, she looked up from her screen. "Right now you are only allowed five level one post-mortem consultations. You have to spend fifty years as a level one without interference before you bump up to a level two ectoplasmic manifestation and are eligible for level three possession rights. Now, sit down, fill out the forms, and I will call you when it's time."

My head was spinning.

I shouted in frustration, "Time for what?!"

She huffed in exasperation. "For your appointment! What, you think you croak and someone automatically guides you around? No.

That takes time, scheduling, and hard work. You haven't even cracked open the manual yet so it'll take even longer. You're going to be a difficult case as it is."

"What manual? No one's given me anything but you and they're forms."

"The handbook that all new spectrals receive. It's right there on the-"

POP!

I jumped back from the puff of smoke that filled the space behind me.

Did I come in like that?

A man was looking about in a daze. He wore a plaid button up shirt and khakis. His hair was slicked to the side with gel and he looked to be in his mid-thirties.

The receptionist shot to her feet, a grin breaking out on her face like a rash. She ripped the headset from her ear, shoved the chair back and raced to the man.

She cried, "Hubert!" and leapt into his arms. She showered his face with loud smacking kisses.

My eyes widened.

They were both fading as was the sound of their kissing until there wasn't anything left.

I spun around looking for them but they were gone, vanished.

My arms dropped to my sides and I huffed, "Sure, she can get out but I can't."

I looked about the room again and my eyes landed on the coffee table where a black book now sat.

That… wasn't there before.

I lifted the weighty tome and read the silver lettering on the plain cover; <u>So, You Finally Died!</u> Underneath it read, "A Guide for the Newly Deceased."

So I just sit here and read this until someone comes, or doesn't?

I groaned and moved behind the desk. The wooden rolling chair looked more comfortable than the worn sofa and at least I might be able to do something besides read the manual.

On the screen was a time table of events; a schedule of different names, places, and times. One appointment, dated for today, was simply titled "Crently House 4:00."

I pulled myself away from the computer to open the manual to the first page.

I was only through the first page of the book when something moved out of the corner of my eye. I lifted my head enough to watch a door fade into existence on the far wall. Was this my way out?

It burst open with a crash.

I jumped and reflexively slapped a hand over my heart, not that it could jump anymore.

An imposing woman was reading from a leather folio.

"Trudy, I need you to change next week's appointment on the tenth to the fifteenth. Then, on that day I need you to change it again to the twenty-seventh. Then, cancel it all together. I need you to pick up the possessed items from box eight and have them delivered to the Melton's by Tuesday. The ecto in sector five is struggling to control his forms and the one in ten, you know the one I mean, won't stop calling and having a nervous breakdown. I need extra back up to Miss. Stone's house immediately and I need everyone to pull back from the Hasting's case. For the meeting tomorrow I need an extra order of spider cider, tea sandwiches, and add an order of imported roach truffles."

I scrambled around the desk and found a notepad and pen in one of the drawers. I could start scribbling the notes down as fast as possible to keep up.

What else was I supposed to do?

"And what time is the meeting today?"

"Umm," I glanced at the screen, "four o'clock at the Crently House."

She looked up from the folio and turned her steely eyes on me.

She was a tall woman of around five foot six, eight in those heels. She wore a venom green suit jacket and knee skirt. Her shoes were a deeper green than the dress. Her blonde hair hung to her shoulders and had high and low lights that were so professionally done one might think they were natural. Even her bangs had been perfectly colored. Her eyes, eyes that would make even the toughest of drill sergeants cower, were a blue so ice cold they could be mistaken for white at a quick glance. The only shield against them were a pair of silver cat eye glasses with black gems in the corners.

I shrank down slightly.

"Who the hell are you?" It was more of a curiosity question than one out of ire which was a relief.

"P-Prudence Lawson."

"Where the hell is Trudy?"

"Umm, some guy showed up and she geeked out. She, kind of, disappeared. I-I don't know where she went."

"Did his name happen to be Hubert?"

I nodded.

Her head fall back and let out what only could be described as a relieved groan. "Well it's about damn time."

I sat up.

That was the last reaction I'd expected.

"Ma'am?"

Her attention returned to the folio. "She's been moping and whining around here for the last thirty years about him. She had an aneurysm young and has been waiting for her husband since. Finally, I don't have to listen to her."

When her eyes came back to me I hesitated before asking, "We-well, maybe you can help me. Where am I?"

She stated matter-of-factly, "You're in the In Between."

"The... In Between?"

"The In Between, Limbo, The Waiting Room, Purgatory, The Other Realm, whatever you want to call it. Most of us call it the In Between."

She snapped the folio shut and ran her eyes up and down my person, making me shudder.

"Well, I suppose you'll do. You're hired. Let's go."

I started. "Hired? Hired for what?"

"Well clearly I need a new assistant." She gestured to where I was sitting. "Trudy is gone and you're all that remains. You took down all my notes, yes?"

"The ones you just said? Yes. I-I have no notes from before that."

"Fine, fine. I don't need old notes anyway." She impatiently snapped her fingers and turned her back to me. "Come on, I don't have all day."

I hurried to my feet and took the pad, pen, and book with me. It wasn't like I had anywhere else to be.

I watched, fascinated, as she pressed her hand to the wall and another door materialized seemingly from nowhere.

Is that all it takes to get out of here? I gotta learn to do that.

As she opened it she said, "Now keep up with me. I move fast, I talk fast, and I get things done fast. Don't lag or you'll be out on your ass faster than you can say *ectoplasmic manifestation*."

"E-excuse me; Trudy called me that earlier. What does that mean, exactly?"

She looked over her shoulder and pulled her glasses off so I got the full effect of her eyes. "It's means, my dear, that you're a ghost. And you better get used to it. I took a quick glance at your file; you'll be here for a long time."

She turned back and stepped through the door.

I quickly rushed after her.

* * *

Book 2 in this series is available – grab your copy today!

Masquerade

a romantically mysterious short story

"Any man tonight who hasn't been watching you is a fool ..."

S. M. Nevermore

Masquerade

The Polish Hall in Uxbridge was decorated to perfection. Black shimmering streamers hung from the center of the ceiling to the windows creating a tent like effect. Tables were covered in deep green tablecloths and each held their own unique centerpieces. In the center of the room, on a table, was an open casket with a skeleton inside. Other haunts and creepers perched on the walls, in windows, and above doorways.

A Touch of Magic had pulled out all of the stops for tonight's Masquerade Ball.

The guests had eaten their fill of the catered food while the DJ started the night off with a jumping chart topper. It was only after their meal, and enjoying a drink or two, that people began to loosen up and make their way to the dance floor. Friends and couples danced in front of the DJ stand where strobe and techno lights played about, around the casket, and near the tables.

She stood back and leaned against the wall, delicately sipping her seabreeze. Her best friend, Marissa, who had been her friend-date to the party, was on the dance floor enjoying herself. When the man, dressed as an aviator, had invited Marissa to dance she had to push her to go. She knew Marissa didn't want to leave her stranded but, at the same time, it wasn't fair to Marissa to keep her chained.

She was into her second drink at this point and was spending a great deal of time crowd watching.

The costumes ranged from funny to historical, heroes to pop culture, and hideous to beautiful. Some of the gowns that the women wore were absolutely stunning. The most popular gowns favored corsets. Each corset piece was adorned differently with gems, embroidery, and metal steampunk pieces.

She ran her hands over the silken velvet of her sapphire gown. The skirt was long and flowed like liquid if she so chose to move from her spot. The bodice was a blue corset with black and silver thread detailing in intricate floral patterns. The sleeves were long bell sleeves of the same material as the skirt. An opal moon charmed collar adorned her neck and opal drop earrings sparkled in the dim light. Half of her brown hair was pulled back in a matching moon clip and the rest hung down her back in ringlets.

She had gone a step further with her mask tonight and had painted it on, finding the typical masks irritating, especially when trying to hide the string among her tresses. She had painted the silver mask and accented with a black filigree design that complemented her emerald eyeshadow.

As she watched the dancers she noted those who were romantic couples and others who were simply friends having a good time. One pair, an older couple probably in their sixties, took to the floor when the song "DJ Got Us Fallin in Love" by Usher came on. Many stopped to watch them tear up the dance floor in a swing style dance that was so well done one would believe it was choreographed. But she knew by looking at them that they were happily in love, had been for many years, and had been dance partners for just as long. It was a joy to watch.

She sighed wistfully.

She looked down at her drink, noting that she had, in fact, finished it a while ago and now the ice was melting. Giving one last look at her friend to make sure she was still enjoying herself, she went to the bar to get another drink.

"Coke, please," she requested. She was driving tonight so she needed to behave from this point on. No more alcohol.

"Sapphires glow brightest in the dark."

The deep voice was unfamiliar to her as was the warm presence behind her.

"And costumes," she said, "don't make corny pick-up lines any less corny." She took a swig her soda and turned around to find herself staring at a broad chest.

Tilting her head up, she found a solid black mask and two blue eyes peering down at her under a black sombrero. Everything from his hat to his boots was black. The cape he wore hung about his shoulders and ended at his calves. The rapier at his side peeked out from beneath it.

"Huh," she mused. "It's not often you see Zorro costumes anymore. He's not as popular as superheroes are."

The man before her smirked and shrugged his shoulders. "He is a superhero, just without all the flash and pizazz that gets a superhero their name."

It was her turn to smirk. "Only tonight this superhero doesn't have a rope to swing from or any damsels to save, pity."

She skirted around him and headed back for her table. She had just set her drink down when a hand took hers and spun her 'round in the direction of the dance floor. Those same hands caught her again and once more she was staring at Zorro's chest.

"Awfully forward and presumptuous aren't you? What if I don't want to dance?"

"I've learned that if I give someone too much time to think they begin to second guess. And if I had asked you to dance you would have thought of a hundred reasons not to. Am I wrong?"

"Well-"

He spun her around and pulled her back again. His painted-on grin was contagious and she returned it.

"If you knew I was going to say no to you then what makes you think I'll let you keep dancing with me?"

"I didn't know you'd say no if I asked. I know you'll keep dancing with me, though. You want to stay in that corner as much as I want to see you in that corner. If you had really not wanted to dance with me, you would have pulled away by now. Besides, no one watches a dance floor like you do and not want to be a part of it."

She couldn't deny the truth in his statement and it unnerved her. "You've been watching me, then."

"Any man tonight who hasn't been watching you is a fool and I pity his blindness."

"Oh," she chuckled, "you're quite the charmer aren't you? Does your costume make you bold?"

"Anyone in costume is bolder. But, I like to believe that I am bold regardless of the mask. I'm sure the same can be said for you, as enchanting without the mask as you are with."

She felt her smile fade.

"I'm sorry," he said, "I seem to be saying the wrong things to you and my last intent was to make you feel uncomfortable."

"No... That's not it."

His smile was gone and was replaced with a look of concern. "May I ask if you had a date to tonight's Ball?"

"My friend." She nodded over to where Marissa was still dancing with her aviator. She seemed completely smitten with him. "It's okay. I'm use to watching from the sidelines."

"You can tell me to get lost any time you like. However, I do hope you'll allow me to be your date for tonight."

"Now why would you want to do that?"

"Like I said before, a jewel like you deserves to be among the other jewels tonight. Let me make this an enchanting evening for you."

His hand was warm on the small of her back and her own hand fit neatly in his. Even as they had been talking he had been leading her in an easy dance that just kept to the beat of the music. She had hardly noticed until the song slowed and he pulled her closer.

She happened to glance behind him at her friend.

Marissa was beaming and giving an enthusiastic thumbs up.

She laughed and shook her head.

He looked over his shoulder, grinned, and then turned his attention back to her.

It was surprisingly easy for him to lead her. Not once did she step on his toes nor did she trip over herself. She was the farthest thing from graceful and had almost no sense of rhythm so the fact that she hadn't maimed him was a miracle in itself.

"You have lovely eyes."

She was brought back to the here and now and looked up at him with surprise. "Thank you."

"A sapphire all over. I am a lucky man tonight."

"Still trying to say all the right things?"

He shrugged while still gripping her hand. "I'm a charmer; did you not say so yourself? And before the night is through you will succumb to those charms."

"I will, will I?"

"Yes. First, we dance. I'm going to let every man here know that *I* am the luckiest man in the room. I only hope you'll continue to give me a chance to win your heart?"

"I'm no damsel in distress in need of saving from a loneliness you think I feel. If this is all in pity-"

She felt her cheeks flush and she cut herself off.

He looked so hopefully at her, so beseechingly, that she lost all train of thought. Whatever thought it had been, it would have only hurt both of them if she'd said it.

This was new territory, never explored by her before. It was embarrassing, and sad, to think such things but it was the truth. She didn't know where to go from here.

The music changed and he didn't miss a beat. He led her into a fast paced tango of moves that left her stomach fluttering and her heart jumping. Her body had no control of itself. Her muscles were only doing as they were asked, not as she had wanted them to. After two numbers he slowed down, tucked her hand in his arm and led her off the floor to her table.

He pulled out the chair for her and quickly sat beside her.

"I know you're no damsel in distress," he said, renewing their conversation from earlier, "nor would I ever wish you to be."

She didn't know why she was so comfortable beside him. Maybe all the dancing had made her addle brained. Maybe it was because he'd seen her.

Really seen her.

"And just what," she asked, "do you wish me to be?"

He insisted without hesitation, "You. I want you to be you and I want you to let me court you tonight since every other man in the room is too stupid and blind to see what they're missing."

"Still trying to say the right things…"

And why did it seem to be working?

He was certainly not like any man she had known or interacted with before. No one today uses words like "courting" or spoke as… poetically. It was as if he were channeling another time and place.

He said softly, "I told you I'm a charmer."

"Are you this way with all the ladies or is this special attention for me alone? Sloppy seconds aren't really my thing."

His eyes never left hers. "The extra effort is yours alone. I'm, in all honesty, never this forward when I've just met a girl." He took her hand and grinned. "Like a magnet, I can't help being attracted to you."

"You haven't even seen my face."

"You haven't seen mine either. But if your face is as lovely as your personality then you're absolutely beautiful."

He couldn't be real. No one, no man, spoke like this to anyone. At least, not in her experience. Was this a dream?

She gave herself a small pinch on the back of her hand and winced.

His brow furrowed in confusion.

She was strong.

She knew that when she had made herself up tonight it had been with the intention of having a good time no matter what happened.

Everything she had done, she had done for herself and no one else; from her dress and mask, from her hair to her shoes. She had done it so she would feel beautiful, elegant, and enchanting.

But, she admitted, some small part of her had hoped that she might earn a little attention. Even if it was only a passing compliment on her dress or her mask.

And yet… was it so hard to believe someone else might see her as beautiful? For just for one night?

He silently watched her, his cheek resting on his closed fist as his arm propped on the table. "I can see the wheels turning."

She shook her head. "Just my own little world."

"Must be fascinating."

"Sometimes."

Why shouldn't she enjoy herself tonight? What possible reason did she have for denying herself innocent fun and flirting?

Would her belief that no one could possibly see her as lovely and pleasant to be with keep her from doing as she had imagined she might do tonight?

No.

Not this time.

She looked into his sky-filled eyes. "Dance with me again."

His smile slowly grew at the corners of his mouth. He got up and offered her his arm and led her once more on to the dance floor. He brought her to the middle of the crowd and put his arm around her.

"Despacito" came on not a moment later.

He beamed down at her. "Ready for some fancy footwork?"

"I'll try to keep up."

"Don't worry. I've got you."

She looked up at him; his eyes glowed behind the mask and she found herself mesmerized. She hushed, "Boy do you ever."

Again her legs had minds of their own. She danced with him like they had danced together every night of their lives and never once did he let go of her hand. Every turn they made, every step they took, brought them back to each other time and time again.

The crowd parted for them. Couples and friends stopped dancing to watch.

She happened to look over and found the older couple from earlier dancing not far away from them. It seemed they had sparked a small dance competition.

He asked, "Shall we give them a run for their money?"

"Let's."

He took her hands in both of his and began a similar swing style dance as the couple beside them.

The cheers coming from the rest of the guests almost blocked out the music.

Each pair gave the other plenty of space to move and the crowd gave them a similar courtesy.

Never had she danced like this before; with a partner so sure or skilled. Never had she trusted someone to lead without her tripping, falling, or causing all kinds of chaos. It was exhilarating.

With the last notes of the song he dipped her and his lips met hers.

He was warm, strong, and held her so firmly.

She returned the kiss and let her eyes droop closed to enjoy the cinnamon taste of him.

The screaming applause went unheard by her ears. Only the thrumming of her heart in her ears resonated when it jumped in delight.

Her arm wrapped around his neck, holding the kiss only a moment longer while he righted. He set her back on her feet and spun her out to face the audience and take their bows.

The DJ lowered the music and stepped to the mike. "Who said Masquerades were a dull affair? A hand for our two couples!"

Cheers went up again and the two couples bowed to each other.

Her cheeks were flushed and her body tingled all over. She waved her hand in front of her face in an attempt at cooling her nerves.

He took her hand and tucked it under his arm. "Let's get some air."

There were other partygoers outside with a similar idea as them to get some air from the excitement inside.

Frost covered the ground and under the moon it sparkled like emeralds waiting to be plucked up to adorn an ear or a neck.

Her breath plumed in the air before her like that of a sleeping dragon, yet her insides felt only the intense chill of the night and she hugged herself.

For a time they stood in silence. He leaned against the corner of the building, arms crossed over his chest.

He broke the silence first. "Penny for your thoughts?"

"Nothing… and everything." She looked at him as if trying to piece together a puzzle that was missing a piece. "Feels like a dream."

He held out his gloved hand and she took it readily. A gentle tug pulled her into his arms where he tucked her close and placed another kiss on her lips.

Her arms wrapped around his back. The cape draped forward and concealed her as his arms circled her waist.

When the kiss broke she rested her forehead against his chest and took a steadying breath, her heart racing.

He softly asked, "What's wrong?" His gloved hand gently pet her head and she, oddly enough, found it soothing.

"Nothing. Absolutely nothing." She laughed sarcastically and gingerly extricated herself from his embrace. She rubbed her temple as she began to pace. "This night is almost too perfect to be real." She turned to look at him imploringly. "Stuff like this… it doesn't happen to girls like me. Ever. So why should I believe any of this is true?"

"Are the men in your life that horrible that you've never heard what I've been saying to you all night?"

Another sarcastic laugh escaped, "First the men in my life should only pass by. Without this mask I'm-"

"Sweet, kind, gentle, and fun to be around."

"You don't even know me!"

"I know enough. We danced together for hours and we've talked. True, we didn't talk about everything or anything but we talked which is more than I can say for a lot of the women I know who are glued to their phones. Besides, you can tell a lot about a person by the way we dance and we dance great together."

She shook her head. "You're-"

"Handsome, suave, sophisticated, charming, enchanting," he paused briefly, his arms crossed again and in the darkness she could see the same smirk gracing his lips. "Stop me at any time you agree with me."

She laughed. She couldn't help it. "Oh... Goddess help me."

"Hey," he pouted, "I'm not that bad. Of all the rakes of the evening you lucked out."

She popped a hand on her hip. "Rakes? Really?"

He mused, "Must be the costume."

"And when the costume comes off?"

"Party!"

She punched his arm. "I'm serious."

He winced and rubbed where she had struck. However, she was sure, he was just humoring her.

His expression softened as he took her hand again and played with her fingers. "When the costume comes off, you are you and I am me. Our lives resume as if nothing had happened. The world won't have stopped turning for one night."

No matter how much they might wish it had.

She whispered, "Do you want it to stop turning?"

"Desperately."

He gave her a gentle pull to bring her back to his arms and give her another kiss. It was a languid, luxurious, and passionate kiss that left her knees weak and her head spinning. She'd *never* been kissed like this. When they pulled apart it was with deep regret on her part.

Something red caught the corner of her eye.

She reached up and slid a rose from behind her ear.

"Where-"

"You're getting cold." He turned her around and gave her a gentle nudge to move her forward. "Inside."

She took a few steps but paused when she looked to the flower. "But where did you-"

She turned.

He was gone.

Not even a trace of his footprints in the ground.

She looked to the rose and lifted it to her nose. The perfume warmed her and she softly smiled as she turned back to the door.

She said into the night, "The world might not stop turning but this better *be continued*."

Keepers of the Crystals - January: Garnet

Steel eyes stared out the window of the top floor of the high rise building. The traffic of the city was a distant sound barely registering in his ears. If he strained he could just hear the honking of horns or the occasional police whistle. But his mind and eyes were in two different worlds. While his eyes took in the familiar night sights, his mind was on times long forgotten.

He reached up to the breast pocket of his suit and felt the rough stone of the pendant which lay within.

The source of his longevity.

When gifted to him, he had set to work learning the myriad of spells and dark magic needed to enhance the stone's magic to extend his life.

It had worked.

But now… now the magic was fading.

In this world of technology, magic was struggling to survive and so was the power in the gem keeping him young and breathing.

Grimacing, he turned away from the window and stormed into the next room of his apartment.

There was nothing in this room, not even a window. He flicked on the light and illuminated the one ornamentation to be seen; if one looked down.

The floor was smooth stone, worn by age, time, and hundreds of feet. Carved in the stone was a perfect circle which was divided, from the center out, into twelve segments. Long forgotten runes ran the circumference of the circle. Each triangular segment bore a roughly cut hole in the center. Surrounding each hole was a pair of constellations, two for each divided piece.

He carefully shut the door behind him. He reached into his pocket, his fingers finding the cord to the pendant. He drew it out and held the stone up to the light. The shard was roughly the size and length of his middle finger and years of worrying the stone had it smoothed to a dagger-like tip. It gleamed bright red in the dim light and throbbed with power.

Tearing his eyes away from the crystal, he gazed down at the circle under his feet. Starting at the top, he counted seven to the right. There, he inserted the stone into the carved slot.

The subdivision rose from the ground and the stone began to glow.

He stood back.

In the empty space his voice echoed back at him, "The others are long dead and buried. But the stones still exist. They would have been passed down if they haven't been lost. Show me where they are."

*****

"I'm open! I'm open!"

The ball whizzed through the air and Jason jumped into the air, angling so the ball smacked into his chest. He let it drop to the ground and kicked it ahead of him.

Dodging other players, he raced for the other end of the field.

A teammate was open and he kicked it to him to make the final goal.

The whistle sounded.

"Good practice, everyone!" the coach called over whoops and hollers. "See you all Saturday for the game. Get plenty of rest."

Jason headed back to the locker room with the rest of the team and quickly changed. He grabbed his car keys from his backpack and dashed to his car.

All of the other students from the high school had left with the busses. A few teammates had parents waiting for them and the rest carpooled or had cars of their own.

Because he had his own car it made life much easier when his parents asked him to pick up his kid sister from their grandparents' house.

He pulled into the driveway and noted that his grandfather's Dodge was missing and only his nana's Nissan remained.

He didn't bother knocking. He opened the door and strode right in to where his sister and nana were sitting at the dining room table working on his sister's homework.

He ruffled his sister's hair as he walked by. "Hey ankle biter."

"Hey!" she wailed and quickly tried to fix her hair.

He went to the fridge and grabbed a soda. As he cracked the top he went back to his nana and kissed her cheek.

She asked, "How was practice today?"

"Fine. Ready for the game on Saturday." He plopped down into the chair next to his sister and looked over her shoulder at her homework. "Ready to go, Kyra?"

"In a minute. Nana's helping me with math."

"Better she than me." He sat back and sipped the soda.

His sister looked a lot like him. Same dark brown hair, same hazel eyes, same sun kissed complexion. Her hair was short, cut at the shoulders with bangs. His hair was short through and spiked at the front.

"Jason," his nana's voice took on a tremor he'd never heard before. "Where's the stone your grandfather gave you?"

Confused by her concern, he reached into his backpack and pulled out the slim blood-red shard. "I just forgot to put it in after practice." He undid the backing of the earring and slid it in place.

The stone was about two inches long. The top part of the gem was wire wrapped to keep it attached to the earring piece and the stone itself came to a sharp point at the bottom.

His nana breathed a sigh of relief and nodded.

He asked, "What's wrong?"

"Nothing, nothing."

Kyra looked at him. "Why do you wear it as an earring? You could do a necklace or a key chain."

"Because grandpa gave it to me as an earring. And, I've been told, it gives me a 'roguish' look."

She giggled. "Roguish?"

"Not my word choice."

"Whose choice was it?"

"The girl's bathroom wall."

"Ew!"

He chuckled. "Come on, Kyra. We gotta let Mojo out and you gotta clean your room like Mom and Dad wanted."

She grimaced, "Awe man!" She shut her folder and started packing her things.

Jason finished his soda and tossed the can in the recycling bin.

"Jason," his nana said softly as she came up next to him, "please be more careful with that earring."

"Nana, I know that it's a family heirloom and Grandpa's super happy to have me wear it. But, it's just an earring. It's nothing special."

"It is to him. And a part of you thinks so, too, or you wouldn't wear it all the time."

He couldn't argue with that. He loved his grandfather dearly and treasured everything the man had given him. The earring came on his sixteenth birthday. His father, strangely enough, was furious with the gift and had spent an hour with his grandfather arguing over it in the other room until they both came out in a huff. Apparently, his grandfather had won because he was able to keep the earring.

It was strange, wearing it, at first. He got a lot of smack from his friends for it but that quickly stopped once the girls in class noticed it. The words, "hot pirate" were in frequent use and it had spurred several of his male classmates to get their ears pierced.

"I promise," he reassured her, "I'll take better care of it and not take it out as often."

"Thank you. Now, let me give you something to take home for dinner tonight."

"Nana-"

But it was too late. She was already halfway in the fridge pulling out leftovers and extras. By the time he was out the door with his sister they had leftover lasagna, salad, and garlic bread.

"Why does Nana send us with so much food?"

Jason shrugged and put the food in the back seat. "I don't know, kid. I think she wants to feed us and clean out her fridge at the same time."

He climbed into the car and started them for home. It was only a ten minute drive; he liked being close to his grandparents.

"How was school, Kyra?"

"Okay, I guess."

"You having any trouble?"

"In math. Mr. Starfus is really tough."

He smiled as he turned on to their street. "I can help you study if you want."

"Yeah?" She rummaged through her backpack and pulled out the paper. "How good are you at variables and fractions?"

"I can hold my own. Tell you what, when we get home I'll shower and then I'll help you with math. Okay?"

"Kay."

"After your math homework, you clean your room."

She grumbled and sunk down in the seat only to pop back up again. "Jason, who's that?"

They pulled into the driveway but he stopped the car at the foot of it.

He had never seen the man before and would certainly remember someone like him.

Tall and lean, he was an older man who easily reached six feet. He wore a black suit with a red tie. His hands rested leisurely on the silver head of an intricately carved walking stick. His skin was a healthy tanned shade and his neatly cropped brown hair was lightly salt and peppered at the temples.

He stared at Jason with eyes the color of a raging storm.

Jason involuntarily shivered.

"Kyra, stay in the car. Lock the door behind me. Get my cell phone and call the police if he takes out a weapon."

Kyra immediately ducked down to the floor where his soccer bag lay. With her hands shaking she fumbled with the zipper.

Jason grabbed his soccer ball from the back seat and stepped out. It wasn't much for defense but it was better than nothing. He firmly shut the door behind him and didn't step away until he heard the distinctive *clatch* of the lock behind him. If anything, his sister was safe.

He stepped away from the car but didn't get any closer to the stranger. "Can I help you?"

The man's eyes looked him over and paused somewhere on his face. His voice was surprisingly deep. "So, you're the new Keeper."

Jason's grip on the ball tightened. This man, whoever he was, intimidated him worse than his algebra teacher. There was an inexplicable power, a shadow, that loomed over Jason the minute the man opened his mouth.

He continued, "There is a slight resemblance, in the eyes."

A resemblance to whom, his father? Was this a business associate of his dad's that he wasn't told was coming over tonight?

Jason tried to keep his voice steady, but even he heard the wavering as he replied, "My father isn't home. If you don't mind, please leave."

The man smirked, "They haven't told you anything, have they?"

A new emotion welled within Jason- irritation. "Who hasn't told me anything? What do you want?"

"I want that earring you so proudly wear."

He reached up and felt the sharp stone. "No way!"

The man heavily sighed. "Stubbornness, that's one trait that never seems to diminish with time." He leveled his gaze at Jason. "Fine. If you won't give it, I'll take it."

The man raised his hand to Jason. A red glow pulsed around his fingers.

Jason's blood chilled and he was frozen to the spot. All rational thought flew from his brain like birds fleeing a wildfire.

A demanding voice shouted in his head, *Move you moron!*

Jason dodged and rolled, keeping the soccer ball clutched under his arm.

A flash of light surged past him, singeing the hairs on his arms as it narrowly missed him.

What the hell was that?

Scorch marks marred the side of the car where he had been standing. But what caused it?

Kyra's eyes were wide and he could see her mouth quivering in terror.

The commanding voice sounded again, *Get him away from your sister.*

He obeyed and leapt to his feet. Keeping the soccer ball tight under his arm he raced away from the car and made a circle to be on the other side of his attacker.

Shot after shot rocketed past him. His back seared with pain as he wasn't quite fast enough to escape unscathed. The tightening, blistering burns licked his ear, his hair, and forced him to zig-zag. He rolled to avoid the shots aimed at his head.

Jason realized, *is he missing on purpose?*

He slid to a stop.

Smoke plumed from the char marks around him. The grass was ruined where it had been hit and even the pavement of the driveway was molten in spots.

The man raised his hand again.

Jason dropped the soccer ball and gave it a vicious kick.

His aim was true. The ball crashed into the attacker's face and knocked him back. Blood gushed from his nose.

A chuckle echoed in his head. *Not bad. Not bad. Simple but effective.*

Desperate barking came from inside the house.

His head whipped around. *Mojo!*

The man pinched his dripping nose with his left hand and aimed another attack with his right.

Jason rushed to the door and yanked it open.

A brown and black blur whizzed past as the German Shepherd aimed himself at the attacker.

Mojo hurled himself into the air, fangs bared to rip into the man's flesh.

Startled, the man blinked out of sight; vanished.

Jason, rooted to his spot in shock, stared at empty space.

Mojo landed neatly on four paws and spun in search of his pray, growling and hackles raised.

The man reappeared at the other end of the driveway, blood oozing between his fingers.

Mojo was on him like lightning, snarling in rage. His teeth grazed the man's leg and closed on empty air. Gone.

Mojo whirled around and charged at the lawn.

Lo, the man appeared again and instantly disappeared.

The steps.

The sidewalk.

Even in a tree the man could not escape the infuriated dog and his razor sharp fangs.

When he appeared again at the head of the driveway Mojo pursued him like a heat seeking missile.

The man thundered, "Enough!"

Mojo lunged.

The man's hand shot out.

Mojo flew, caught in his attacker's magic, through the air and careened into the side of the car hard enough to make it rock.

He fell to the ground with a whine and didn't get up.

Kyra screamed, "Mojo!"

Jason's head whipped around. "Kyra, stay in the car!"

But it was too late. Kyra was already scrambling out of the car and racing to the poor dog, tears streaming down her face. Panic for her friend overshadowed her fear for herself.

The man rolled his eyes, wiping the last of the blood from his nose. "You're going to make this difficult, aren't you? Just hand over the stone and I'll be on my way."

Jason knew it was stupid to refuse.

Not with Kyra's life at risk.

Not with his own life equally at risk.

He couldn't win and, above all, needed to protect his little sister.

A gnawing feeling grew in the pit of his stomach. Giving up the stone would save them both. So what if it was an heirloom; this was an emergency. Surely his grandfather would understand.

So why; why wouldn't his hands move to remove the earring? Why did every ounce of his being forbid him from turning it over to this monster?

The man growled in anger; Jason's hair stood up on end at the sound.

But then, suddenly, the man smiled. And, if anything, the sinister shine in the man's eyes was worse. The man said, "You want to be the hero? Then we'll give you something to sacrifice for."

He took a step toward the car. His hand raised to point straight at Kyra.

Kyra's eyes went wide in panic. She wrapped her arms around Mojo, desperately trying to lug him to safety. She barely budged him an inch.

Shocked awareness rose in Jason. This wasn't just a threat. The man would actually do it.

He yelled, "Don't you dare hurt her!"

The man smiled. "It's your decision. Hand over the stone or your sister dies for your senseless pride."

He knew without a shadow of a doubt that he could not give the stone to this man. He would not.

His sister's eyes streamed tears as she pulled with all her strength on Mojo's limp form.

The stranger's lips curled into a sneer, and his fingers began to glow –

Jason cried out in anguish, "All right!" He threw up his hands in surrender. "I'll give it to you! Just don't hurt my sister!"

The man's snicker was edged with malice. "Smart boy."

Jason's hands felt as heavy as lead, but he forced himself to reach up. He willed his fingers to undo the clasp on the back of the earring.

And just what do you think you're doing, boy?

Saving my sister.

And you think giving him the stone will save her?

I don't see much choice.

Idiot!

Jason winced. *What do you propose I do?*

What the hell was he doing?

He was losing his mind. Panic was making him hear voices in his head.

Use me!

To his amazement, the stone that he had worn for years suddenly burst with ruby-red light; as if a star were being born before him.

His eyes watered from the bright sting.

Okay, kid, I'm taking over.

His arms thrust out of their own accord.

Heat pulsed down his arms and into his hands. Unlike the man before him, this heat didn't blast out like a sci-fi movie. It morphed and changed until it formed the shape of a longbow.

His left hand reached back and he felt something warm and soft on his fingertips. Grasping it, he pulled forward a glowing arrow and notched it.

The man's triumphant grin turned into a scowl of fury. His hand erupted in fire.

Jason's anger at the man released as he loosed the arrow.

It flew and shot straight through the man's hand.

The stranger howled in agony and staggered back, gripping his hand to his chest. The wound smoldered and smoked but didn't bleed.

Go boy!

Jason hurried in front of his sister and blocked her from view.

The man's free hand was gripping the cane like a vice. He looked between his hand and the cane as if battling an unanswerable riddle.

Finally, he looked at Jason.

"Don't be a fool, kid. Give me the stone and I'll leave both of you alone."

He's lying. I told you, don't trust him.

"No. You're not getting it."

"Then die."

The ground shook.

Cracks broke through the driveway.

The stranger's injured hand arose with new flames. But Jason could see the effort was causing him pain.

Hands up, boy!

Jason threw up both hands.

Jason's arms surged with energy. In a flash, a tall war-door shield loomed before them.

The fire-blast slammed into the shield; angry flames licked around its edges.

The shield glowed brighter, brighter, and Jason wrenched his eyes shut against the pain.

At last it seemed as if the brightness dimmed. Jason carefully opened his eyes and peered around the edge of the shield.

The stranger's breaths were coming in ragged heaves. He leaned heavily against the cane. His gaze was murderous. "Count your blessings. Next time, I won't let you get away with this."

He raised the cane and brought it down with a resounding *crack*!

He vanished.

Jason's shield slowly disintegrated, leaving no trace of it behind on his hands.

He stared, open mouthed, and wondered if he'd seen what he actually saw. A rational part of his brain told him that he had gotten hit in the head at soccer practice and was probably unconscious on his way to the hospital. Another part argued that it was very real, evident by the burn marks all over the yard and the fierce tingling in his arms.

"Jason," came a small whimper behind him.

He spun around and saw Kyra, wide eyed and shaking while still clinging to their dog.

"Get in the car, Kyra."

"But-"

He barked, "Now!"

She sprang to her feet and hurried around to the other side of the car. She yanked open the door and climbed inside.

Jason's second thoughts were for his dog.

He opened the back door on his side and gingerly picked up Mojo. Unsure of where exactly the dog was injured, he tried not to wrangle him as he slid him onto the back seat.

By the time he got in the driver's seat Kyra had climbed over the center console and was in the back seat cradling Mojo's head in her lap.

Jason snapped, "Kyra, get back up here this minute."

She didn't even lift her head to look at him.

He turned on the engine when he got no reply and sighed, "Fine. Buckle up."

She twisted herself enough to grab the buckle and clip it around her body. One hand remained on Mojo at all times and when she was secure all attention was on the unconscious dog.

The moment the snap was done, he was squealing the tires in reverse, jamming the car into gear, and racing down the road.

He ignored almost all driving laws to get to where he needed to be. Only when they got close to his grandparents' house did he slow to pull into the driveway. Relief flooded his nerves when he spotted his grandfather's truck.

He sprang from the car and ran to get Mojo, all the while screaming, "Grandpa! Nana!"

The front door flung open and his nana stood frozen, her jaw dropped. When she regained her composure she shouted, "Frank! Frank! Hurry!"

She hustled down the stairs and jogged to Kyra who was getting out of the car. Kyra was wrapped in a tight hug and started sobbing.

Jason managed to get the large dog out from the back seat as his grandfather came sprinting down the stairs.

He shouted, "What happened?"

"Some freak with a pyro complex tried to kill us."

He caught sight of his grandparents shooting each other a look. His grandfather urged him inside while looking up and down the street. Jason got Mojo inside and set him down on the sofa.

Kyra's lip quivered as she looked at the dog. Their nana kept her close as their grandfather came in and got down to examine the dog.

Jason asked, "Think he'll be okay? He was only protecting us."

His Grandfather said nothing as he gingerly felt the dog's head, shoulders, back, and hind legs. "This is a damn good dog, risking his life to save you two. And he's lucky I'm a damn good vet." He opened one of the dog's eyes to look at him and checked inside his mouth. "This dog is as tough as nails. On first inspection, there doesn't appear to be anything seriously wrong. My humble opinion is that he should recover but we'll keep a close eye on him."

Jason sighed and sank back onto the sofa.

New tears leaked down Kyra's face as she cried in relief.

"He's a bit banged up," his Grandfather continued, "he can rest up here for the night. I'll check on him tomorrow and take him to the clinic to get him thoroughly checked. I might be retired but the new vet still lets me use the clinic when I need to." He gave the dog's ears a good scratch. "We'll have some chicken waiting for him when he wakes up. He's earned it."

"Kyra," Nana said softly, "let's go get a bowl of water for Mojo. He'll be thirsty when he wakes up and we can get that chicken in the oven for him."

She nodded and allowed herself to be steered into the kitchen.

His Grandfather sat down in his reclining chair and looked at him expectantly. "Start at the beginning."

And he did.

He described how he had come to pick up Kyra after practice, their drive home, and their encounter with the freak in their driveway.

"And, I know this is going to sound crazy, Grandpa, but the- the stone it... talked to me." Wow, it even sounded insane now.

"Of course it did."

Jason almost fell off the couch. "What?"

"Jason, I was hoping that we wouldn't have to have this particular talk." He leaned forward, braced his elbows on his knees and clasped his hands together. "Believe me, your father should be giving you the same lecture I gave him when he was your age. But, the situation has changed."

"What lecture?"

Tell that old codger that if he gets the story wrong, again, I'm taking over.

Jason winced. He reflexively reached up and felt the stone. His grandfather gave him a knowing look.

"If he keeps mouthing off to you, tell him to shove it. Back talk is the only language that jerk understands."

Tell that old fart-

"Agh!" Jason had had enough. He undid the earring and threw it onto the coffee table. "Here! You two have it out. I'm not doing this."

His grandfather looked at the stone longingly. He reached out and picked it up, holding it like a baby chick. Reflection, regret, and fondness flashed across his face as he stroked the shard.

"Unfortunately," he said, "this stone won't speak to me anymore. As much as I'd relish hearing that Jackass again, my time is done. As soon as your father was born the stone's power began to fade from me. By the time he turned fifteen the voice was barely a whisper. And, when he turned eighteen, it went silent all together."

"Dad never said-"

"Your father never heard the voice. He never felt the call of the stone. Oh, he adored the tales I told him as a child." He smiled wistfully. "But your father's mind grew more… analytical as he grew up. He lived on facts, numbers, and charts. He no longer needed magic. When I passed the stone onto him I had hoped he might hear it during his reckless teenage years. But he was never in enough danger to awaken the stone's powers. He returned it to me, saying it was childish to hold onto fairy tales. He even went on to say that he wasn't going to fill you and your sister's heads with stories that had no basis in reality."

His eyes misted and he quickly wiped them dry. "I'd never known such hurt, not since my own dad passed on."

Jason listened, transfixed. He'd never thought about how different his dad and grandfather were, until now. They were night and day. Where his grandfather had always entertained him with stories of knights, dragons, and even played such games with him as a child, his dad had focused on games that developed skills. Math, science, and English were the only "recreations" his father encouraged other than Jason's interested in soccer. But never once had they played a game that they made up off the tops of their heads. Not even with the train set where Jason pretended that the engines could talk.

His grandfather pulled himself out of his dwellings, holding the stone up to catch the light. "But, when I learned that he was expecting you, I knew that I would do right by you and make sure that you inherited this gift. Oh, your father was furious when I gave this to you. However, I'm still his father. He gave in when I said that he had every right to give up family heirlooms and the same choice would be given to you."

"You said," Jason interjected thoughtfully, "that Dad hadn't been in enough danger to awaken the stone. Does that mean that you…?"

"When I was sixteen I took my new car out of town where the local kids liked to race. I was young and stupid. I raced the guy with the fastest car and took a corner too sharply. I flipped the car. It's only thanks to this stone that I'm alive today."

"So when that guy attacked us earlier-"

"Yep. It lies dormant until the life of the Keeper is threatened. When it's woken up, it stays awake until a new Keeper is born."

"That's what that guy called me before. What does it mean?"

"The Keepers are an order that are sworn to protect the crystals and the Earth from dark magic. Magic that, I fear, is going to be unleashed."

"By that creep that tried to fry me?"

"The very one."

"Who is he?"

"I think that question is better asked of him." He motioned to the crystal and tossed it back to Jason. Jason caught it and put it back in his ear; it immediately began talking to him.

At least the man grew some sense in his old age. Get comfy, kid, we have a lot to talk about.

Jason did as he was asked. His grandfather got up, gave him a reassuring pat on the shoulder, and went into the kitchen. Jason stroked Mojo's head as he closed his eyes.

We have existed since time immemorial. It was man's first ancestors that discovered us. Until that time, we lay in the Earth keeping the balance of nature in check. When man found us, he put us to use to learn, grow, and evolve. After that, we pop up throughout history; the temples of Egypt, the tribes of the Americas, even the North and South Poles. However, it wasn't until a time of great hope that we were collected. Only one man was strong enough to accomplish such a feat; Merlin.

It was like listening to his grandfather's stories as a child. This world, this past, came to life behind his closed eyes.

Merlin believed that our gifts could be honed and used for the greater good of all man-kind. So, he called for us and we answered his power. In turn, he gave one of us to twelve of the most trusted Knights of the Round Table. I am the stone of protection and he entrusted me to one whose heart yearned to shield others from those that would wish them harm. Each stone was unique and Merlin chose a knight who embodied a trait that best fit the stone he was given.

Merlin never expected one of the Knights to betray us.

Jason asked, *Lancelot?*

No, boy, and don't interrupt me again. No, it was not Lancelot. This knight's name was Frederick. He inherited the ruby stone, the stone of vitality. Its traits would keep a person youthful and healthy into their senior years and aid others in living their best lives. Frederick saw the stone as a way to extend *his life, to become immortal. Well, unknown to us, Frederick began searching through Merlin's books, practicing dark and forbidden magic. This allowed* him to bind the stone to him and him alone; he was able to increase the stone's power to extend his life for centuries.

Wait a minute, Jason jumped in, *so that man that attacked us, the one that almost killed us, that was-*

Boy, do you ever follow directions? Don't interrupt again. He sighed, *Frederick. Yes. And, I suspect, that his hold on the stone is weakening. In this modern world there's little room for magic. Because of this, the ruby's powers are fading. And if they fade to what they once were, Frederick will die. Well, there's no doubt that he wouldn't just stand around and let that happen. To return the stone to the strength he needs to continue his existence, Frederick is now seeking out the other crystals. When he reunites them, infinite power will be his. You were the first stop on his long list of Keepers.*

Jason had a dozen questions but he held them back.

Okay, I'm finished. Speak.

Who are the other Keepers? Where are the crystals? How did they get them? How do we warn them? Will he come back and try to kill me again? What does-

Enough! One at a time. I can see you're going to be a slow learner.

Jason bit back his retort.

The other crystals and their Keepers are scattered, he continued. *I'm not sure where all of them are. Each crystal was passed down from the Knights to their descendants. After so many centuries, who knows where everyone has migrated to or died off. Most likely, Frederick will come back for me when he's collected a few more and increased his power. I don't think he anticipated my strength after being so newly woken. We were fortunate he only had his own crystal. Right now he's retreated with his tail between his legs and this will give us time to find the others.*

Us?

Yes, us. It's your job as a Keeper and my job as a crystal. If I concentrate hard enough, I can catch a faint trace of the Amethyst stone not too far from here.

I don't have a choice, do I?

Afraid not. Not if you don't want to die, put your family at risk, or be responsible for the deaths of other Keepers such as yourself.

Jason groaned and rubbed his eyes. When he opened them, his grandparents and sister were watching him.

His nana smiled, "I packed you some food in a cooler to get you started."

His grandfather said, "Go home and pack a bag. Only the essentials, nothing more."

His sister whined, "How come he gets to go save the world and not me? Why don't I get a crystal, too?"

Their grandfather chuckled and affectionately ruffled her hair. "Had you been first born you would have. But, this is your brother's responsibility."

Tears welled in her eyes. "I want to go, too."

Jason tenderly admonished, "No way, ankle biter. Not this time."

She ran forward and crashed into his arms.

He said, "I'll be back soon."

"Promise?"

"Promise." He stood up and set her down on the floor. He gave his nana a hug and a kiss goodbye then his grandfather led him outside. "You going to tell Dad?"

"I'll tell him. He'll hate me for it and you'll most likely get a hundred calls from him. You do what you have to do. Even if I wanted to stop you, you're eighteen and can do as you like."

Jason looked at the car. "I don't know if I can do this."

"Jason, today you risked your life to save your sister from a man who wished you both dead. If you can stare death in the face, nothing is impossible." He gave Jason's shoulder a slap and squeezed it reassuringly. "I'm the luckiest man in the world to have you as a grandson."

Jason gave him a sideways look and a wary smirk. "Would you hate me if I refused to go?"

His eyes shadowed and Jason's smile faded. "Jason, Frederick won't be satisfied with just one stone. In order for him to restore his own crystal's strength, he must gather all twelve. The reason Frederick didn't kill you and just take the stone is because it must be freely given. Yours is the stone of protection. He knew that this stone would be the hardest to acquire because the stone would never let you give it up. It would defend to the end."

Jason hesitated, "And if he manages to get them?"

"The stones will be drained of their power until there is only one; his. He will be the ultimate power. Governments will fall at his feet and the world will crumble."

Ice cold shivered down Jason's back.

"Jason, Frederick is not a stupid man nor a rash man. He'll calculate every encounter. If he can't convince the Keepers to hand over their crystals, he'll try to convince them to join him. If they don't, he'll destroy everything they love until he gets what he wants; just as he tried to do today."

Jason tilted his head back and stared at the endless expanse of sky. "I'm not a hero."

"Yes, you are, Jason. You stood between your sister and death; if that doesn't make you a hero then nothing will. If I could I would take on this responsibility for you but this job was given to you, not I; not your father. If we tried to face Frederick we'd end up like poor Mojo. And I know you would never ask your sister to take your place, would you?"

Jason shook his head.

"We're your Achilles heel. Our job is to stay home and protect the family as best we can. He's tried to get to you once; by searching for the other Keepers you reduce the chances of him coming back. Stay home and hide, he'll most surely come back and kill us all."

"I… I don't want to do this alone."

"You won't be. Find the Keepers, join forces. Together, you'll defeat that demon of a man. Alone, you'll all perish." He turned Jason to face him, both hands gripping his shoulders in a vice grip. "I believe in you, Jason. You've always been strong and you've always taken my lessons to heart. You can do this. Just like the rest of us, you were chosen. You were born into our family for a reason and this is it. Do what Garnet says and trust your gut."

Jason smirked. "Garnet? Is that his name?"

"It's easier than calling him Jackass every five minutes."

I heard that.

Jason shook it away and looked down as his grandfather pulled something from his wallet. It was a credit card with Jason's name on it.

"I had this account transferred to you the day you were born. There's enough to get you through if you spend wisely."

Jason took the card and tapped it on the tips of his fingers. "You planned for this?"

"The account was my fathers, then mine, then it was your father's, now it's yours. I had prayed this day would never come. But, here we are."

Jason slipped the card into his back pocket.

His grandfather grabbed him and pulled him into a bear hug that he readily returned, not quite ready to let go. When it could be prolonged no longer, his grandfather patted his back, sniffed, and released him.

"Now, go on, you got a centuries'-old devil to vanquish."

"Yes, sir."

He got into the car and buckled up.

So, Garnet.

Mhm?

Where's the Amethyst stone?

Start the car and I'll show you.

******

Frederick stumbled into his penthouse and staggered through. He managed to get to the next room without falling or breaking anything. He was furious enough that even his hand felt like a distant memory of agony.

He pressed a hidden button on his cane and the silver head popped off, revealing the glowing Ruby. He withdrew it and slipped it into the stone slot where it belonged.

Frederick looked down at his black hand, the remaining injuries from that damned arrow.

How could the Garnet stone have done this much damage when it had been dormant for so long? Even if every generation had awoken the stone, there was no need for its full power so how did it still have all of it now; now, in this world, while his stone continued to grow cold and die?

He growled and clenched his fist, igniting fresh pain. It would need healing before he could continue his search.

He looked to the glowing ruby, safe in its cradle of cold earth.

"Show me the next one."

A Villainous Comeback: Envy

Preface-

For every story told there are characters.

Most villains embody a major flaw that defines who they are in the story, just as heroes embody a major virtue.

When a villain reaches the end of their tale, they are absorbed by their flaw and forever remain in a white void of emptiness. Their hero counterparts move on to a place of comfort and contentment.

There is no escaping fate.

Is there?

~~~~~~~~~~~~~~~~

"I can't take this anymore!" A shadow surged from the genie lamp in an eruption of grey smoke, gold eyes blazing.

A pair of emerald eyes stared into a reflection-less gilt mirror that floated as if it hung on a wall. "Calm yourself, Greed."

"Well, we can't all be as calm as you, Your Highness," he snarled. "Go back to looking for your reflection in that mirror, Envy. One of these times you might finally find a wart."

She seethed, "Why you-"

A female voice with crimson eyes shouted, "Would you two knock it off?" The nautilus shell necklace that hung from her neck glowed and throbbed red like a disembodied heartbeat.

Envy growled, "No one asked you, Wrath."

A fourth shadow grew to loom over them and ordered, "Enough, all of you." Purple eyes stared them down, pupils dilated in controlled anger. When the three went silent the shadow slowly returned to its original size.

Greed started again, "I'm tired of being stuck in this void. Pride, you promised to find a way out yet here we remain."

Envy sighed wistfully, "When a story ends we absorb all of the character's magic but this place hinders the magic we gather. We can't use it to its full potential."

"And," Greed added, "While we waste away the centuries here, the heroes are living happily and free."

Pride was calm as she answered, "Worry no more. I believe I've discerned a way to free ourselves." The long staff she carried had a dragon claw top with a faintly glowing emerald gripped in its claws. "I have not been sitting idle all this time."

Envy looked away from her mirror. "Oh?"

Wrath seemed to calm and crossed his arms over his chest. "Do tell."

"The stories were told and there's nothing we can do about it. However, if we were to be freed of the void and destroyed the stories all together-"

Greed finished, "Then we would be free now and forever."

"Exactly! All we need to do is find the original pen and ink manuscripts, the ones that gave us life. Once destroyed, the memory of the tale will be removed from every human that has ever heard it. The Virtues will be oblivious to our deceptions. Not only that, but if we destroy them without the Virtues knowing, they'll be destroyed as well. Humans underestimate just how much tales affect who they are. With the Virtues gone, humans will descend into their baser sins and we will control their every move. The world will be ours."

"And just how do we accomplish such a task?"

"There's the hitch," she said. "We ourselves cannot leave this place; we all know this. But, if we can get a human, an everyday person, to accept our... gifts, we might be able to slither our way into their bodies."

Wrath asked, "And by 'gifts,' just what exactly do you mean?"

Pride walked over to Envy and held out her hands. "Your mirror."

Envy quickly backed away and blocked the mirror. "What do you want with my mirror?"

"You'll see."

"No!"

Greed snarled, "I want out; let her do what needs to be done."

When Envy refused to budge he darted forward like a snake, grabbed her arm, and yanked her away from the mirror.

Envy's wail of despair was ear splitting.

Pride ignored her as she went to the mirror. With the tip of her staff, she gently tapped the bottom of the glass and a perfect circle was cut. The piece then floated to her outstretched hand.

Envy screamed in rage but Pride ignored her again as she covered the glass fragment with both hands.

There was a flash of light.

Greed released Envy and she stumbled forward to examine the object Pride held; a silver compact mirror, ornately decorated with scroll work on the lid.

Envy whimpered, "What did you do to my mirror?"

"I made it better." She grinned. "This lovely, unassuming mirror will entice the vain to look into its depths."

She opened the compact and held it out to Envy who snatched it. As she gazed inside she purred in delight.

"However, it's the self-conscious, jealous one who will be able to wield the piece." She took the compact away from Envy who sniveled. "You'll be free of this plane once they accept the darkness."

Greed and Wrath came forward to examine the mirror.

Greed was skeptical. "How are you getting into the real world?"

Pride waved her hand before the larger mirror. The surface rippled like a pond before it eventually stilled.

The mirror now contained a moving image.

Dozens of people mixed and mingled about on a large expanse of grass, eating, reading or talking to others. Trees were scattered about and behind it all was a large red brick building with hundreds of windows gleaming in the sunlight.

Wrath crooned, "So many unsuspecting souls."

"Indeed," Envy agreed. "And what a strange land."

Greed asked, "This is the real world?"

"Yes," said Pride. "A world filled with little known magic except for that found in books. However, once we get there we'll be able to harness all the hidden magic this world has to offer. If all goes well, we'll all escape. Then," she smirked, "the fun can begin. And, I think I found our first accomplice."

She stepped back away from the mirror, the other three moving behind her.

She said to the compact in her hand. "Magic mirror, serve us well."

She drew back her arm and threw the compact at the mirror.

It sailed through the portal and dropped into the path of a very unsuspecting human.

~~~~~~~~~~~~~~~~~~

"Do you understand now, Terry?"

"I think so." However, his handsome face was scrunched up in confusion. "How do you understand all of this, Dana? It's not even English."

"Shakespeare *is* modern English."

"Bull!"

"No, it's true. It's modern English."

"Well, whatever English it is, if it weren't for Thee, I'd be failing."

She giggled, "Not bad."

"Well, either way, thanks for helping."

He stretched out his long, jean clad legs and lay back on the grass, his arms behind his head. He was wearing a white t-shirt but didn't seem to care about possible grass stains or grass getting in his short cropped black hair. With the summer now here, Dana noticed that his skin had started to get some color to it.

"No problem. Anyway-"

"Ugh!"

A disgusted grunt made them turn to look at the enraged female charging her way across the green towards them. She was tall and thin, wearing short shorts and a tank top. She had straight waist length black hair and porcelain skin.

"You break our lunch date to hang with this nerd?"

Terry sat up. "Courtney, be nice. You know I need to study for finals."

"What's more important, finals or me?"

Terry opened and shut his mouth several times but didn't actually say anything.

"RGH!" Courtney stomped her foot and stormed away.

"Courtney, wait!" he called as he shoved his book in his bag. "Sorry, Dana. Thanks again," he said before darting off after the fuming girl.

He caught up to Courtney and Dana watched him trying to rationalize with her.

A perky voice made her turn.

"Hi, Dana!"

A pretty girl with bright blue eyes beamed as she drew closer. She wore a pink t-shirt and a white denim skirt that stopped at her knees. Her blonde hair hung past her shoulder in large country curls that reminded Dana of Carrie Underwood. The ideal all American girl. She was even dating the all American football star on the varsity team.

Dana stood up and brushed off her pants, "Hey, Maddie."

As best friends they were polar opposites. While Maddie preferred pinks, whites, and lace, Dana preferred blacks, purples, and leather. Maddie loved chick flicks and romances while Dana stood in line for the Dead Pool movie. Maddie listened to hip-hop; Dana blasted rock. They were a mixed set.

"What's the princess upset about now?" Maddie asked as they watched the couple bickering.

"Terry studying for finals with me rather than keeping a lunch date with her."

"What is she so threatened by? He needs to study and it's not like he's going to leave her. She's got some sort of spell on him. Spending time with you isn't going to change his mind. I mean-" She flushed in embarrassment, realizing what she'd just said. "Well, you two have been friends since kindergarten. Doesn't he see you as a little sister, or something? I mean- I... I'll stop talking now."

Dana smiled softly and shouldered her bag. "It's okay, Maddie, I get it."

"I'm sorry, Dana."

"Don't be sorry. It'll be okay."

"You sure?"

"Yeah, I have more important things to worry about anyway. Finals; you know?"

"He'll come around, Dana," she said confidently.

"How do you know?"

She shrugged. "I just do. He'll see through her and on the other side will be you."

"How do you always know the right thing to say?"

Maddie beamed. "A gift. She," she pointed to Courtney, "has her powers." She pointed to herself. "I have mine. Now, I'm going to meet Brandon for practice. Want to come?"

"Thanks, but no thanks. I need to use my break period to get some work done. The library is always quiet about this time."

Maddie gave her a quick hug and, literally, skipped off toward the football field.

Dana shook her head and smiled. However, this faded as she walked past Terry and Courtney. Now that they'd made up, Courtney was making it publicly known.

Why don't you just lift your leg and pee on him? she thought bitterly as she went inside.

Rather than go straight to the library, she went to the bathroom. Luckily, it was empty so she locked the door and went to the mirror.

She didn't see anything wrong with herself when she saw her reflection. She saw an average girl, maybe a bit on the short side, with pale skin and auburn hair that liked to frizz in the summer heat. Brown eyes that, hidden behind black glasses, appeared a bit bruised from long nights of school work. She sported piercings on her ears and a diamond stud in her nose.

So she wasn't model thin. So she didn't have porcelain skin that glowed.

So, how was it that a demon like Courtney got everything I'd been wanting since middle school?

Dana knew that answer.

It was because Courtney was beautiful.

It's not fair! She slammed her fist against the sink. *I knew him first. I'm better than she is. Why can't he see that?*

She observed at her reflection and took a shaky breath.

She had to stay calm lest tears make an unscheduled appearance.

Reaching into her bag, she pulled out her makeup and touched up her eyeliner.

She did a double take.

For a moment, however brief, she thought the mirror had moved. The glass itself seemed to... wave.

"I'm studying too hard," she muttered to herself, putting her things away and turning from the mirror to leave.

WOOSH-

WHAM-

"Ow!"

Clatter!

She doubled over from the blinding pain and tightly gripped the back of her head.

A few feet away from her, something gleamed.

When the pain faded, she crawled over and picked up what she assumed to be the object that assaulted her.

The silver disc was heavy and filled the palm of her hand. She popped the clasp and discovered two mirrors inside. The lid itself was beautifully done in shining silver with mother of pearl filigree work that gave it an antique feel despite it being so shiny new.

But where did it come from?

She looked at the bathroom mirror and shook her head.

No. Someone could have thrown it in through the open window.

The bathroom door rattled and she quickly slid the compact into her bag. She made sure she had everything in her bag before opening the door. She apologized to the two girls wanting to get in, claiming she hadn't heard it lock behind her. She moved past them and made her way to the library to finish studying.

The next day at school was similar to the one before. Only, this time, Terry assured her that Courtney wouldn't be interrupting them like that again. However, he was still feeling the pressure.

He groaned, "My brain... Fried... Go on without me..." He flopped over the picnic table and twitched a few times for dramatic effect.

Dana scolded halfheartedly and poked him with her pencil. "Big baby. Sit up, you have work to do. Come on, *Of Mice and Men*."

"Okay, okay, umm... Main characters-"

"Hi, guys!" Maddie plopped down on the bench beside Dana and set her bag down. "Hitting the books hard?"

Terry grumbled, "No, but I'd like to."

Dana chanted, "Characters, write, now."

He dropped his pencil, took Maddie's hands in his, and dreamily gazed into her eyes. Maddie quirked an eyebrow and quickly darted a confused glance at Dana.

"Oh, Maddie," he swooned, "Light of my life, distraction of studies, marry me and forever keep me from holding another text book."

Dana and Maddie fell into a fit of giggles. Maddie freed a hand only to fan her flushed face.

"Oh, you," she laughed. Terry released her other hand and she continued, "Well, I don't know how you can study. Dana makes a far better distraction than I."

Dana quit laughing and shot her a sharp look which Maddie quickly avoided.

Terry didn't seem to notice as he returned to his notes. "Yeah, she is."

Dana's face flushed.

Maddie stifled a small chuckle and turned to Dana. "Did anyone claim it?"

"No. I went to the office but no one had reported it missing."

Maddie said, "You'd figure if it was stolen someone would be looking for it."

Dana nodded. "I know, but no one's claimed it yet."

Terry reached over and waved a hand between the two of them until they noticed him. "What are you two talking about?"

Dana went into her bag, withdrew the compact mirror and handed it to him. After examining it for a moment he set it down.

"If someone lost it, I'd think they'd be scrambling to get it back. It's real silver."

Maddie asked, "How do you know?"

"Heat conductivity and the way it sounds when you tap it. Mother of Pearl isn't nearly as expensive but it does add character to the design."

Maddie shot Dana a questioning look.

She answered, "His parents are jewelers."

"Ah," realization dawned on her. "You're sure it's real silver?"

He smirked, "I learned how to tell real silver from fake silver before I learned how to crawl."

Dana rubbed the back of her head. "It sure felt like real silver."

Terry's eyes widened, "Someone threw it at you? Well, no wonder no one reported it. It's an assault weapon." He leaned over the table and tried to look at the back of Dana's head. "I thought your head looked unusually lumpy today."

She laughed and pushed him away, "Shut up."

"Well," said a rather bitter voice, "Isn't this a cheery bunch?"

If Terry heard the acid in Courtney's voice he didn't mention it.

"Hey, babe, you're early."

Like a cobra, she slid onto the bench beside Terry and looped an arm possessively through his. "I was so bored!"

"We should be done in a minute." He turned his attention back to Dana. "Anything else I need to study?"

"The notes I gave you should cover most of everything. I gave you the study questions and I want your responses by Friday."

"Ugh," Courtney grimaced, "She sounds like a teacher."

Dana's eyes narrowed and thought, *"she" is right here.*

Courtney's eyes fell on the mirror and her eyes glittered. Before Dana could make a grab for it, Courtney snatched it.

"Who's is this?" she asked and opened the mirror to look at her reflection.

Terry answered, "Dana's."

"*Yours?*" Her eyes peered over the silver to give her a mock once over. "Why would you need a mirror?" She purred, "I doubt you've ever really looked in one before."

"Courtney-" Terry started.

"EEK!"

Maddie and Terry jumped.

She dropped the mirror with a clatter and Dana hastily took it back.

Terry asked frantically, "What's wrong?"

"I-I-I thought- I thought I saw-"

She scrambled through her bag, pulled out her cellphone and switched it to selfie mode. After a moment's examination she sighed and put it down.

"Babe, everything okay?"

"I thought I saw a pimple." She turned to him. "Can we go now? Being around nerds is making me see things."

"Courtney-"

"Now!" She grabbed his arm and dragged him off.

Maddie mocked, "Yeah, because hanging out with nerds makes you grow pimples."

"In her head, we're the cause of every school disaster known to man. I mean, without nerds they wouldn't be expected to get good grades. Everything would be a beauty contest." Dana flipped her hair back and batted her eye lashes at Maddie who pretended to faint.

Despite the rough treatment from Courtney, the mirror appeared unscathed.

She stared into her eyes' reflection and could have sworn they changed from brown to green.

Trick of the light.

~~~~~~~~~~~~~~~~~~~~

"Dana! Dana! Dana!"

She peered around her locker door at Maddie who was doing a fantastic imitation of a kangaroo.

"Yes, Maddie?"

"Did you hear about Courtney?"

She shut her locker. "No, what happened?"

"Well, she-" Maddie paused and leaned in close to Dana.

When it became borderline uncomfortable Dana asked, "What?"

"Your skin looks gorgeous. Your pimples are gone. What've you been using?"

Dana felt her face flush. "Nothing. I woke up like this."

It had been as much of a surprise to her as it was to Maddie. Dana had almost screamed when she looked in the mirror that morning.

"Wow. Anyway," she finally backed off, "Courtney's on a rampage and ready to kill anyone in her path. Come on!"

She grabbed Dana's hand and started dragging her down the hall. Dana struggled to keep up and stumbled several times as they rounded the corner.

"Ma-Maddie, since when do you care?"

"You're my best friend and I love you. I felt you needed to see this."

She slammed to a halt and yanked Dana forward.

Courtney's pained voice came from behind her locker door. "My life is over! I can't believe this!"

She was surrounded by her three friends, triplets Cassy, Chrissy and Carrey. The school knew them as The Four C's. They were doing their best to console Courtney but she was near hysterics. Even Terry was failing to comfort her.

"Courtney," he started, "they're only a few pimples. It's no big deal."

"No big deal?" She turned on him in a boiling rage. "My face looks like a pizza."

"It does not. It's just zits. Everyone gets them. They'll go away."

Her eyes narrowed. "I'm not everyone."

Chrissy asked, "Did you try a new product?"

Cassy asked, "Have you tried cover up?"

Carrey asked, "When did this start?"

Courtney snapped, "Would you three zip it? I saw the first one when I looked in some nerd's mirror."

Dana stiffened. Her hand automatically went to her pocket and pulled out the mirror.

It has to be a coincidence.

"*That* nerd."

Her head snapped up to see Courtney pointing an accusing finger in her direction.

Terry's body went rigid. He said tightly, "That *nerd* is my friend."

"Don't be ridiculous, Terry."

"Courtney, knock it off."

"Terry, she's a nerd. You have more important, more popular, obligations."

"You know what-"

"If this doesn't clear up we are so not going to the dance."

"What does it matter what you look like as long as we have a good time?"

"Who cares what I- Ugh. Do you even hear yourself? Of course it matters." She slammed her locker with a loud *BANG*. "Stop hanging out with nerds, Terry. You're starting to sound like one."

"You can't tell me what to do, Courtney."

"I'm your girlfriend; you do as I say."

"No, you're not."

There was a collective gasp from the sizeable crowd they'd gathered.

Courtney stepped back, her fists clenched. "What did you say?"

"You heard me. I'm so sick of you putting people down. You're self-centered, selfish, and more concerned about your looks than about us. We're through." He turned his back to her and headed for Dana and Maddie.

Courtney released what could only be described as a roar and ran to the nearest girl's room.

When Terry reached them Maddie gave him a hug.

She asked, "You okay?"

"Surprisingly enough, yeah."

Before Dana could say anything, Chrissy approached them and pointed to Dana's hand.

"Is that the mirror?"

Dana said, nervously, "Yes."

"Can I see it?"

Reluctantly, she handed it over and Chrissy opened it to look inside.

Like her sisters, she was tall with tan skin and blonde hair. The biggest difference between her and her sisters was that Chrissy had long, lush eyelashes. Dana felt a sharp pang of jealousy.

"Where did you get it?"

"It was given to me." Not a lie per se. It was given to her, all right; she still had the bump to prove it.

Chrissy's brows furrowed and she did a double blink, shook her head and handed it back.

"Something wrong?" Dana asked.

"No, I thought I saw something but I was wrong." She turned and followed her sisters into the bathroom where Courtney was hiding.

Dana opened the mirror and glimpsed at her reflection.

Those startling gem eyes flashed for the briefest of seconds.

Terry's strong arm draped over her shoulders, pulling her out of her thoughts.

"So, ladies," he had one arm around each of them, "care to join a poor bachelor for lunch on such a lovely day?"

Maddie smiled brightly, "Sure."

Terry pleadingly looked at Dana and she, too, smiled. "Sounds great."

As they walked along she caught him peering down at her face. "What?"

"Are you using something new? Your skin cleared up. It looks nice."

She blushed.

"What do you think, Pride?"

"Envy, before the week is out, you'll have a new body."

Envy did a pirouette in front of the mirror and regarded her own featureless reflection.

"A new body. I'll have a face again."

She waved her hand before the mirror to reveal the face of the girl, still tightly clutching the mirror.

"Yes," Pride purred. "She's tasted the magic and will soon be addicted to it. The more she uses the mirror, the more influence you will have on her."

Greed stood to the side. "I don't know," he chimed in. "She doesn't seem to get it."

Pride waved him off. "A temporary thing. Don't worry. She's seen what the mirror can do even if she doesn't quite understand it yet. It will work, give it time."

Envy huffed in exasperation, "If I must."

She regarded the mirror once more, her fingers itching. She could only imagine what freedom tasted like.

Anticipation tasted like bitter apples.

Dana stared into the mirror.

Glared at it, really.

She'd woken up this morning to find that her eyelashes, normally in desperate need of mascara, were long and full without the application of chemical cosmetics.

"What are you?"

The eyes that stared back at her were her own but she had seen someone else's twice now.

She was a practical girl. Just because she'd read *Harry Potter* didn't mean she believed in magic.

And yet, how else could she explain the changes that had come over her?

Her skin had cleared up overnight and now her lashes had grown and thickened.

As much as she had wanted to stay home and figure out what was going on, she needed to be in school.

It was as she sat through history class that she turned the mirror over and over in her hand, pondering whether she was crazy or not, thinking the way she was.

So far I've been given Courtney's skin and Chrissy's lashes. If this thing had something to do with that, what else can it do?

Tap.

Tap.

Tap.

Tap.

One of The Four C's, Carrey, was sitting a row in front of her by the windows and was tapping her long nails on her desk. Long, strong, and beautiful compared to Dana's own brittle, bitten stubs.

She glanced around.

No one was paying any mind to her.

She looked at the mirror.

She looked at her classmate still tapping away.

Opening the mirror, she aimed it at Carrey.

I want her nails, give them to me. Give them to me, now!

After a few moments she pulled the mirror back and expectantly peeked into it. A few seconds passed.

Nothing.

She quickly snapped it shut and buried her face in her hands.

What am I doing? She wondered in disbelief. *I'm asking a mirror, an inanimate object, to give me long nails. How pathetic can I be?*

The bell rang and she got up to pack her bag.

Crack.

"Ow!"

She turned to look at Carrey.

Someone asked, "You okay?"

"Yeah," she said and held up her hand. "I broke my nail." And she had, down to the quick.

Dana looked down at her hands and watched as her nails grew before her eyes.

She quickly hid her hands and busied herself packing her bag. It wasn't until everyone, including the teacher, was gone that she stood by her desk. Her hand shook as she opened the mirror.

Sharp, strange, emerald eyes stared knowingly at her.

Dana glanced around to be sure no one was around and nervously whispered, "What are you?"

"I am what you've always wanted."

She sank down into her chair, fearing she might pass out. "What?"

"I can give you everything you've ever dreamed of."

"Everything?" Her fear slowly slipped away and was replaced by an unfamiliar amount of curiosity. "How?"

"You know exactly how. You've already seen what I can do."

She knew she shouldn't be taking from others just so she could get what she wanted.

It was wrong.

But Terry had finally begun to notice her more. Her skin, her eyes, he'd already complimented both. He was finally seeing her as a girl and not just his childhood friend.

At last, she said, "All right," and shut the mirror with a resounding *click*.

Over the next few days she collected more and more attributes that she craved.

No.

Needed.

The more she used the mirror, the faster the process happened, she noticed. All she had to do was aim the mirror and will it to happen.

Every day was a new compliment from Terry.

Every day was more time spent with him.

Every day, she was getting more and more of what she coveted.

~~~~~~~~~~~~

"Look; my hand!"

Envy held out her hand for them to see.

It had begun to fade away and was almost transparent now. The shadow that was Envy was beginning to disappear.

Pride said, "You're starting to transfer into her body. The more she uses your magic the more you will become her. It won't be long now."

~~~~~~~~~~~~

"Hey, Dana? Can I talk to you for a second?"

Dana, checking her makeup in the mirror, snapped the mirror shut and turned to Maddie. She didn't know why she bothered looking into the mirror anymore. Her skin was gorgeous and she didn't need to wear excessive makeup to hide anything.

"Sure, what's up?"

Maddie sat across from Dana. The library was busy with many students doing last minute studying. "You know you're my best friend, right?"

"Yes."

"And, you know everything I say to you is out of love; even if it hurts?"

Dana quirked an eyebrow and responded slowly, "Yes."

"Good. The thing is, you've... changed, recently."

Dana crossed her arms over her chest. "Changed?"

"Well, for one thing, look at your clothes."

"What's wrong with my clothes?"

"Since when do you wear colors? What happened to your corsets and rock tees?"

"I was tired of them so I found these." She gestured to her blue lace camisole.

"And the skirt? You always wear Tripp pants."

"It's a high-low skirt. What's wrong with it?"

"You're not wearing your favorite black eye shadow or any eyeliner. When was the last time you wore your purple lipstick? You even took out your piercings. And you're not wearing your glasses anymore."

"Contacts." A lie- she'd taken perfect eyesight from another student. Then she growled, "Since when was it crap on my life day?"

It was getting harder and harder to keep her voice level. Had they not been in the library she would be shouting.

"I'm not crapping on your life, Dana. You've changed. You went from not caring about what you looked like to constantly looking at yourself. Ever since you got that mirror-"

"Enough!" Her fist clenched the mirror until her knuckles turned white and the clasp bit into her palm. "Keep your nose out of my business and leave me alone."

"Dana, what's gotten into you?" She reached out to take it but Dana held it behind her back.

"Nothing- will you let it go?" The hurt in her friend's eyes made her soften. She took a deep breath and said, "I'm sorry. I didn't mean to snap like that. I just decided to make some changes for myself."

"For yourself? Dana, are you really doing this for you or is it for-"

"Hey, Dana."

Both girls looked up at Terry.

He asked, "Ready to go to lunch?" He shot a smile at Maddie. "Hi, Maddie."

"Hi, Terry," she said softly.

Dana slid her stuff into her backpack and held onto the mirror as she took Terry's arm. "Yes," she said, "I'm ready for lunch." Dana tugged him out of the library and relaxed once they were outside.

"Did you two have a fight?"

"What? No. Just a disagreement." She kept her arm looped in his as they headed for the picnic tables.

"About?"

"My clothes. She doesn't do well with change."

"Well, why did you so suddenly decide to wear colors? You've always liked black."

"Yeah, and I do. I just decided to try something new." She released him so they could sit at the table. "What do you think of my clothes?"

"Well, I've always liked black on you. But, you look pretty in any color."

"You're so sweet." She peered deeply into his eyes and batted her lashes. "Terry," she asked.

His face took on a stunned, stupid, countenance which pleased her. It was the same expression she had seen him give Courtney one too many times. "Yes?"

Innocently, she asked, "Wasn't there something you wanted to ask me?"

"Ask you?"

"Uh-huh." While holding his hand she traced patterns on the back of it. "You know, about a certain event happening? The one on Friday?"

"O-oh, yeah." His cheeks suddenly flushed; his grin was sheepish and nervous. "Would you go to the dance with me, Dana?"

She beamed. "I thought you'd never ask. I'd love to."

Finally, things are going my way.

That night she went to the mall to get what she needed for the dance. When she returned home she tried on the dress she bought. She couldn't help smiling.

The blood red dress hugged her in just the right way. The skirt itself reached her knees and flowed when she spun. The off shoulder straps gave her a sultry look she'd never known before.

The only fault in her plan was-

"Maddie." She glared into the full length mirror. "She could blow the whistle on me."

She paced around her bedroom. She had to do something to keep Maddie from interfering. But...

"I could never hurt her. She's my best friend."

"Why not?"

She strode to her purse, pulled out the compact and opened it. "What?"

"Why not hurt her?"

She gaped appallingly at the mirror. "I can't!"

"But you can do something."

"I can?"

The eyes appeared amused. *"Of course. Everyone is envious about their friends for something."*

She pictured her friend in her mind's eye and the one thing that always jumped out at her was-

"Her hair."

She moved back in front of the mirror and lifted one of her locks. Though shiny, it still frizzed in the humidity and would curl unevenly even after straightening. She could never get the voluminous, bouncy curls that her friend always had.

"Whatever it takes."

She snapped the mirror shut.

~~~~~~~~~~~~~~~~~~

"So close. I can taste it."

~~~~~~~~~~~~~~~~~~

The school grounds had been decorated for a night of dancing. A temporary dance floor had been set up in front of the D.J. stand. The picnic tables had been moved back to make room and additional tables had been added to accommodate the number of people.

Chinese lanterns were strung between the trees for an unearthly glow but brighter lights had been set up around the dance floor for the dancers. A refreshment table was placed far back behind the picnic tables and was laden with treats.

Dana drank it all in while being led on Terry's arm. She reached down to tentatively double check the small shoulder bag at her side for the pocket mirror.

She knew for a fact that it was there but fear of losing it made her check over and over again.

"You look beautiful."

She tore her eyes from her bag to look up at Terry who was gazing down at her with a charming smile.

Her cheeks flamed. "Yeah?"

"Yeah."

He led her toward a picnic table and she sat down, being mindful of her dress. "Why don't I go get us some drinks and snacks before we dance?"

"Okay."

As soon as he walked away she pulled out the mirror.

Every hair was in place and every lash was curled. Her lips were glossed and her skin glowed under the moon light.

"Happy?" The jade eyes sparkled in amusement.

"Very."

"You'll be even happier when you take from Maddie."

Dana's face fell. "I-I don't know." Her resolve weakened the more she thought about it.

"You have to."

"But, why?"

"Once you have all you want from others he'll never be able to break your spell."

"But-"

"It's either that or have everything ruined. Look."

Dana peered over at the refreshment table to find Maddie talking urgently to Terry who was shaking his head no. It seemed Maddie wasn't letting him go without hearing her out.

Resolve returned, she shut the compact and made a bee line for the refreshment table.

"Terry, would I be saying anything if I weren't worried? Come on, you have to have noticed something off about her."

Dana crossed her arms over her chest and glared at the back of Maddie's head. She hissed, "Off about who?"

Maddie whirled around with a surprised squeak. "Dana," she smiled awkwardly. "We were just-"

"I know," she growled. She looped an arm through one of Maddie's and dragged her away.

In a secluded spot, away from prying eyes, she spun Maddie around to face her.

"How dare you," she fumed.

Maddie paled, "Dana, what's gotten into you?"

"Nothing has gotten into me!"

"Dana," she insisted. "Look at yourself. Why are you doing this? You didn't need to do this to get Terry's attention."

"Okay, stop." Her fists clenched at her sides, body shaking with fury. "For one thing, it's my choice whether or not to change. I changed for me; not everything is about boys. For once I wanted to be fairest of them all."

"Dana-"

"And who are you to criticize?" She thrust the mirror into Maddie's hands. "Look at yourself. If appearances didn't matter, you wouldn't have gotten your hair done or be wearing makeup."

As soon as Maddie looked into the mirror Dana made her wish. But, almost immediately after looking into it Maddie shut it and gave it back to Dana.

"It's one thing to change over time but this is ridiculous! I don't even know you anymore."

"Maybe you never did," she snapped and walked away.

Once she was away from Maddie she opened the mirror expectantly.

Nothing.

Before she could ask what went wrong, arms circled her waist from behind.

"There you are," Terry said. "Want to dance?"

She smiled up at him and put the mirror away. "Absolutely."

He took her hand and twirled her onto the dance floor.

Finally, everything she'd ever wanted was hers.

Terry held her while they swayed.

Dana's eyes never left his.

Her skin prickled.

Her head began to swim.

She staggered and he swiftly drew her closer to keep her from falling.

"Dana, you okay?"

When the world stopped spinning, Envy's green eyes gazed up at him. "I'm just fine."

Freedom tastes like gooseberry pie.

The Kept Wolf

"Tundra, I'm home!"

Arya shut the door behind her as she heard the *click clack* of claws hitting the wood floor.

She put down her purse, shucked off her jacket, and got down to greet her dog. She didn't have to get down low; he wasn't small by any means.

She didn't know what breed he was. To her, he looked to be a husky mix. He had the coloring of a gray husky and the gorgeous blue eyes associated with the breed but he was massive.

The dog whined and licked her face while his tail wagged happily.

"Okay, okay, I missed you, too."

She stood up and scratched behind his ears then went to put her things away. As usual, he followed her into the bedroom and sat while she got organized and changed into her sweats.

With a groan, she flopped onto the bed.

Tundra hopped up beside her and stretched out across her stomach.

She laughed and scratched under his chin. "Ugh, what a day. You'd think working in a bookstore would be easy. I had one customer who argued with me for half an hour that twenty percent off of the sign price should be the new price when the price listed *was* the twenty percent off price. And one woman got upset because I couldn't put a book on hold because it was a new release and I had only a limited supply of them. I wasn't going to deny someone else the book when this woman might not come back for a month to get it. My feet are screaming."

One of the best parts about having a dog was that she could talk to him for hours and he wouldn't think she was crazy. He listened to her no matter what she had to say, even if it only made sense to her.

"Well, another day done. How about some dinner?"

Tundra let out three loud barks then got up and jumped off the bed.

Arya could call herself a spoiling parent based on the way she treated her dog. He ate a good portion of what she prepared for herself.

Tonight, she broiled a steak, cooked mashed potatoes and steamed some carrots. She cut the steak in half, cooked Tundra's to medium rare, and set it aside while hers finished cooking. She set his bowl down and took her plate to the table.

She watched him eat and shook her head.

She'd tried numerous dog foods. The pet store was ready to throttle her after the tenth bag he refused to eat. She had to keep giving him human food to make sure he ate. In the end, she'd relented to her dog's wishes and gave him the food he wanted.

He seemed happy.

That was all that mattered to her.

When she finished eating she did the dishes, took a long hot bath and climbed into bed with a book.

Tundra joined her on the bed, rested his head on the pillow next to hers, and dozed.

Arya lazily stroked his fur while she finished the chapter. When she finished she shut the book, set it on her night stand, and clicked off the light. She snuggled close to Tundra and fell into her dreams.

She's beautiful.

He watched her sleep and made sure she was peaceful. He then slipped out from under her arm and silently padding out of the room.

Safely in the living room, he began the painful procedure of shifting.

Bones snapped in and out of place, muscles contracted and expanded, and the hair that covered his body began to disappear.

He had to take some time to steady himself once discomfort ceased.

He then reached under the sofa and withdrew a t-shirt and jeans. He pulled them on and, once decent, went back to the bedroom.

He gingerly sat himself down on the edge of the bed, careful not to wake her.

Gently, he reached out and stroked her brown hair, now silver in the moonlight. During the day he was mesmerized by her pale skin and amber eyes. She had a soft smile that always warmed him.

Who else would have welcomed in a potentially dangerous stray?

It was her scent that had first captivated him.

He remembered every detail.

He'd been walking back to his car with every intention of heading home. He'd passed the book shop and the most alluring scent hit him like a ton of bricks. His body took over and before he knew where he was or what he was doing, he was in the store watching *her* ring up a purchase.

He hadn't even been sure it was her he was smelling.

He picked up the first book he could reach and brought it to the register. As she rung up his purchase, so close, he confirmed his nose's hypothesis.

It was her.

It was a split second decision to leave the shop, throw the book into his car, and duck behind the nearest building to change. So reckless was he that he had finished his shift when it dawned on him to look for prying eyes.

Shame on me.

Desperation was no excuse for forgetting everything he learned at birth.

The patience to wait for her to close the shop for the night was the hardest thing he'd ever done. But when she did, he kept his distance as he followed her car on her short ride home.

Her scent trailed behind her and hit his sensitive nose like a warm piece of chocolate cake. He wanted that scent forever.

When they reached her house he acted on a gambler's impulse. He whined.

She'd turned to see what had made the sound.

He stepped forward, head bowed, tail drooped, ears flat and eyes pleading.

For a moment, time stood still. They merely looked at each other, her in shock at the sight before her and he floored at his own actions.

What am I doing?

"Where did you come from?"

Her voice had dragged him out of his thoughts and his ears perked forward.

Slowly, she inched toward him and he whined again. "Are you lost?"

His tail slowly wagged as she got closer. She offered her hand for smelling and he did so merely to let her know that he was friendly.

He butted his head into her hand.

She began to scratch behind his ears and sat down on the steps leading to her door.

So soft!

Her hands were silky and warm as they pet him. Her fingers ran through his thick fur with ease and he knew she was checking for a collar.

"Well," she said, "no collar. You must be looking for a place to stay."

He looked up at her and his tail wagged faster.

"Come on." She got up and clapped for him to come, which he did.

After that it was history.

It had already been over a month since he made the choice to be her pet. On nice days she put him out in the fenced-in backyard for the day. On rainy, or overly hot days, he stayed inside for shelter.

While she was gone he shifted and did what he had to as a human from her house. He kept his clothes and cell phone hidden and only retrieved them when she was gone. He'd made calls to the necessary people to let them know he was alive and well but told them not to look for him. And at night, well, at night he changed.

Looking at her in human form was far different from wolf form. For one thing she was in color. And the moonlight peeking in on her through the window was an image that could only be appreciated as a human.

If he could be sure not to lose his mind to the beast inside, he would stay a dog forever to be with her. But, being human kept his mind human. Stay a wolf too long and you become the wolf.

She was a heavy sleeper; not even a hurricane could wake her up. And she was so used to his other form's routine of getting on and off the bed that it hardly ever woke her anymore.

Was he still cautious?

Always.

She mumbled incoherently in her sleep and he sighed.

For now, this was as close as he could get without terrifying her.

Eight o'clock on the dot, Tundra's nose pressed under the blankets to get at her neck. The cold always shocked her awake but she was quick to pull the blankets over her head and block him out.

He whined and pawed at the blankets until he finally found a way in then proceeded to crawl under the blankets and lay beside her. He nudged her face with his nose and whined again.

Who needs an alarm when you have a dog?

"Okay, okay, I'm up." She stretched and draped an arm over her dog. "Party pooper," she said and nuzzled against him. "Ugh...Just want to stay in bed all day."

But, she knew that was an impossibility. She pushed the blankets off and swung herself out of bed.

He followed her into the kitchen and sat obediently as he waited for breakfast. Ever polite, Tundra waited for her to sit to eat before he started on his own food.

He was full of surprises.

He was so intelligent that sometimes she had to remind herself that he was a dog. There were some days that she swore he understood more than just a few commands. When she talked, it was as if he actually listened to what she said, not simply waiting for attention.

She cleaned her bowl from breakfast and went to dress for the day. Tundra followed shortly behind her and continued to do so as she went about her morning routine. He watched her do her hair, put on her makeup, and even brush her teeth.

"Don't you have anything better to do than stare at me all morning?" she teased and ruffled his ears.

He wagged his tail.

"All right, come on," she said and opened the back door for him to go outside. She made sure there was water in his bowl before she gave him another pat. "Behave yourself." She shut the door, grabbed her purse, and went out the front door to her car.

Even though she knew he would be fine on his own for the day, and never cause any trouble, she was always nervous about leaving him home alone. Many times she'd thought about bringing him to the bookstore and keeping him with her. But it wouldn't work. A big dog like that would only cause problems and a few of her customers might be less than tolerant. It was best to leave him home even if she worried like an overprotective parent.

~~~~~~~~~~

He had to admit; his level of patience was increasing every day.

He waited until she was gone for at least a half an hour before shifting form. He knew all of the neighbors' routines and was able to calculate exactly when they'd leave and when they'd return.

First, he went under the deck via a hole and retrieved the second set of clothes he'd stored there. When he came out, he shifted, pulled them on, and then located the spare key she kept under a flower pot. He let himself in and his body relaxed when the door shut behind him.

With a sigh, he sat himself down on the sofa and pulled his cell phone out of his jean pocket. There was only one number other than his own that he knew by heart. He dialed it and it was answered on the first ring.

"Well, look who's alive. Still enjoying being a pampered pet?" The voice busted out laughing on the other end of the phone line.

He growled, "Stuff it, Adrian,"

"Don't get pissy with me, Ryker. Remember, I'm the only one keeping things calm on this end."

"All right, all right. Just tell me what I need to know."

"The pack elders keep asking where you are."

"And?"

"And I tell them I don't know. They know I'm lying. They tell me to tell you that they want you back, now."

"Well, too bad. I'm not a pup anymore; they can't order me around."

"No, but they *can* order *me* around. Ryker, you're the alpha. I'm not fit to run the pack. You need to get home yesterday."

"I'm not leaving."

"You have to at some point. You've been on good terms with the elders for three hundred years. I'd hate to see what they do when you piss them off. If you don't want to be a danger to that girl then you'd best get your ass home."

Ryker's voice was low, just barely a growl. "Are you ordering me, Adrian?"

"No, I'm telling you what you already know but refuse to do."

"Is that all?"

"No, Tiana's been hounding me for the past two weeks wanting to know where you are."

He sat up straight on the sofa. "What did you tell her?"

"Nothing. I told her the same thing as I did the elders. However, she's much more persistent than them."

"I'll bet. The last thing I need is her pounding on the door." Tiana would kill Arya should she ever get the chance to get her claws on her.

"What are you going to do?"

"Keep her at bay. I'm not interested. And I need you to run interference for me in the meantime."

"She's slated to be your mate. The elders decided that when you two were born."

"I'm old enough to decide whom I'll take for a mate and when I'm ready."

"And the girl you're with now?"

"What about her?"

"Are you planning on mating with her? I've never known you to so desperately try to stay with a woman before. Are you just playing pet or are you thinking about taking that forever step?"

The idea had crossed his mind. But how could he do something like that to her? How could he ask her to leave her life and her world only to be shoved into his? It wasn't fair to her.

Not to mention the sensitive fact that her dog was a *werewolf*.

"I haven't decided what to do, yet. For now, I'm staying here. This is the most relaxed I've felt in years."

"Enjoy yourself. Make sure she gets a rawhide chewy for you."

Before he could snap at his brother he heard a peal of laughter and then the line went dead.

He cussed under his breath and tossed the phone aside.

That was all he needed, the elders and an angry she-wolf on his tail. He knew he would have to go back home eventually. But doing so would be taking him away from Arya and the life he'd started to build here. If he left, he knew she wouldn't recover easily.

He saw the love and care she put into cleaning the area around a small tombstone in the backyard belonging to a cat that had passed away some years ago. Every time she went to tend to it she cried, as if reliving the loss anew. He couldn't, in good conscience, add another loss to her memories.

If he left, he would only be hurting her.

He leaned back and stared up at the ceiling.

Damned if I do, damned if I don't.

If he stayed, the pack elders, or Tiana, would come after him and, consequently, Arya. If he left, it would be like ripping her heart out, losing another pet and never knowing if he'd died or got lost. He ached whenever he saw her go to that tiny grave site. He wouldn't be able to live with himself knowing that he would be the source of her tears.

For now, he'd stay put.

Besides, he was as attached to her as she was to him.

Normally, he would spend his day lounging and relaxing. While he was a pet, there were no responsibilities. However, if something wasn't working and needed repairs, he would do it while she was at work. She was always pleasantly surprised when something suddenly started working again, or better than it was before, and it made him happy to do it for her. But most days, like today, ran smoothly and he was able to quiet his mind, relax his body, and enjoy his time away from the pack.

His phone vibrated at quarter to five, meaning it was time to shift back before she and any of the neighbors came home. He stripped out of his clothes and opened the back door just enough so that it could be pushed open with his nose and lock behind him.

The change itself was less painful, and much faster, the closer to the full moon it was. Unfortunately for him, the full moon was last week. He had been smart to give himself those fifteen minutes to change. By the time his bones, muscles and joints settled into place he was weak and tired.

One thing about being a shifter, it never got easier; even with age.

He picked up his clothes in his mouth, pushed open the back door and let it shut behind him. He found the hole under the deck and pushed his clothes far enough that no one would see. He pulled himself out just in time to hear her car pull up into the driveway.

He sat quietly on the back porch until the door opened and he was let inside.

Arya opened the door and got down to pet and hug Tundra. He was panting and wagging his tail as he was let inside after a long day. He whined and licked her face.

"Easy, boy, I'm home now."

He seemed frantic, almost like he hadn't been sure she'd come home. Never had she come home and had him react this way.

She stood up and led him back into the house to start dinner. He stayed glued to her side, which made it a problem as she moved about the kitchen getting what she needed to make dinner.

"Oof, Tundra, you're too big to be doing this," she said, referring to his wrapping himself around her legs over and over again. Finally, she pointed to the corner of the kitchen. "Go lie down."

He glanced at the corner, back at her, then at the corner again.

She could have sworn she heard him sigh as he did as he was told.

Free of the wandering dog, she turned back to finish dinner.

She was filling their plates when her doorbell rang.

After she made sure Tundra was eating, she went to the front door and opened it. If it was a friend or relative she didn't need them getting scared by the large, but loving, dog. He could be startling at first glance. She knew she'd been startled the first time, thinking he had been a wolf.

What was waiting at the door was most definitely not family and certainly not a friend by any means.

"Michael." She crossed her arms over her chest and firmly planted herself in his way. "What are you doing here?"

Tall and lean, Michael had always been attractive. Blond, blue eyed, swimmer's build, and an easy going smile that could lure anyone in. It did for her. She'd been instantly attracted to him and drawn in by his charms. A fatal mistake she'd paid for later in their relationship.

"I think I left my good sneakers here. I only came to get them."

"You left nothing here and even if you did I would have thrown it on the front lawn."

"Oh, come on, Arya. Let me in. I want to talk."

"No."

"Why not?"

"Why not? You really need to ask? Get lost."

He tried to take a step in but she blocked his path.

"We were good together, Arya," he crooned. "There's no reason we can't be again."

He had always been a sweet talker. He could get out of all kinds of trouble with those baby blues and that voice.

"No. You cheated on me! Not even if you were the last man on Earth would I take you back."

His expression grew dark and his voice lost that syrupy edge. "No one dumps me. No one makes a fool out of me. Let me in or I'll-"

"Grrrrrrrrr."

Arya was pushed aside by Tundra who had come out of nowhere to stalk Michael like prey.

Ears back, claws out, hackles raised, and canines bared, he was scarier than any wolf she'd seen on television. Animal Planet had nothing on this.

Were his fangs always that long?

Michael yelped and staggered back, gripping the rail to keep from falling down the stairs. "Where the hell did *that* come from?"

"*That* is my dog."

"Call it off! Looks like a freakin' wolf."

"He's not a wolf, he's a dog. And he's the sweetest dog I've ever had."

"Sweet my ass. Look at him; he's practically foaming at the mouth."

Tundra was still growling and stepped forward with a deliberate slowness that was both threatening and terrifying. She'd never seen Tundra growl before. Was Michael that much of a threat? Dogs were a good judge of character. If Tundra felt that Michael was someone to be warry of, maybe she should be more concerned about what might've happened had Tundra not been there.

"Call him off," Michael shouted as he backed down, "he's rabid."

"He's not rabid," Arya smirked, "he just doesn't like you." Her smile faded. "And neither do I. Now get off my property before I call the police."

"This isn't over yet. Not until I say it is. No one breaks up with me and gets away with it."

Tundra released a bark so loud it even made Arya jump. Michael scrambled down the remaining stairs and took off down the street.

Once gone, Tundra's demeanor changed in an instant. His tail wagged and he returned to her side, looking up at her. If she hadn't known any better, she'd think he was smirking. But that was ridiculous. Dog didn't smirk, not really, and he had only done it to protect his pack; her.

Boy did she need protecting.

Who knew what Michael would be capable of when he was furious? She'd never seen him get that angry before. Not even when she first kicked him out of the house and threw all of his things onto the front yard.

Tundra woofed softly to get her attention back to him and she reached down to scratch behind his ears. His tail thumped on the deck.

"All right, you earned an extra helping tonight."

Seeming proud of himself, his tail and head held high, he trotted back into the kitchen.

Arya chuckled as she shut and locked the door.

This dog... He was something else.

~~~~~~~~~~~~

A boyfriend.

An ex-boyfriend.

That was one thing he hadn't counted on.

He sensed no love between Arya and Michael. At least, not on her end. All he could smell from Michael was rage.

He had more than enough reason to stay now. Not simply to be by her side, but to protect her. There was no doubt in his mind that Michael would make good on that promise. Michael might have done something then and there had it not been for the intervention.

He hadn't wanted to scare Arya, but it was the only way to protect her. She seemed pleased by his actions.

She was fine with a dog protecting her.

But what about a werewolf?

He went back into the kitchen with her and enjoyed the meal they shared. An added bonus to his taking up residence with her-she was a fantastic cook.

The rest of the night progressed much the same as it normally did. They ate, she showered, and they went to bed.

He wondered if she allowed him into her bed out of loneliness. It couldn't have been that long ago that she and Michael had broken up. Maybe having him beside her was a way to help her recover from the emotional trauma.

Well, whatever she needed, he would give it to her.

While she read her book, the T.V. on as background noise, he kept his head in her lap and relished the attention. He only woke from his dozing when she began turning everything off for the night.

As she fell asleep, he reaffirmed his earlier thoughts.

He would protect her.

The following day he was put outside as per usual and he waited patiently before getting his clothes and changing.

Today's routine would be different.

He walked into town and began a stakeout around the bookshop. Now that he knew of Michael's existence, he didn't want to take any chances. Not with Arya's safety as the main concern. He hoped the boy was smart enough to not do anything during the day but he would err on the side of caution.

He went to his car, got his wallet, then went to the small cafe across the street.

He sat outside under an umbrella and ordered a coffee and a newspaper. The first sip was heaven. He hadn't had coffee once since meeting Arya and he had missed it more than he'd realized.

Using paper and coffee as a guise, he quietly watched the book shop.

For two hours he sat at that table keeping an eye on things. It was a quiet day but the town was still bustling with people and cars.

After taking advantage of the shop's bottomless coffee for so long, he decided it was time to move on. He left a very generous tip for his waitress, folded the paper for the next person and walked across the street to the book shop.

What better way to keep an eye on things than to be in the center of the attraction?

A bell chimed as he walked in and the smell of incense burning assaulted his sensitive nose. Though not unpleasant, the sandalwood was too strong for him.

"Welcome."

Behind the counter, Arya looked up from pricing books to smile at him.

His mind went blank.

Arya asked him, "Can I help you find something?"

It took him a second to find his tongue to answer. "No, no, just browsing." He started to wander between the rows of books.

There were several other customers in the store. A mother was sitting in the corner reading a book to her daughter. An elderly couple was perusing the cook books and a lone teenager was in the sci-fi section. He himself slipped into the fiction section, grabbed the first book he laid his hand on and opened it to "read" the jacket.

For the next hour he picked up random books in the fiction section and pretended to read the jackets. Many customers slipped in and out and some stayed for about as long as he did, simply enjoying the atmosphere.

Arya was ever the gracious hostess. She smiled at every customer, happily rung up purchases and showed patrons where to find things. Every person knew her and she knew most of them, as was common in such a small town.

It didn't look like Michael was going to show his face today. *Good.*

The book he'd had in his hand for the last twenty minutes he brought up to the counter for Arya to ring up.

She asked, "Did you find everything okay?"

"Yeah, thanks."

He watched her ring up the purchase and bag it. He handed over his credit card for her to swipe and signed the receipt.

"You seem awfully familiar. Have we met somewhere?"

His hand stopped mid swipe to cross his Ts.

"I've been in the store before," he said and finished signing.

"No, I feel like it was somewhere else."

She was watching him, examining him really. He slid the pen and paper back to her and she finally focused her attention on the register and not on him. She handed him a piece of paper with his copy of the receipt.

He asked, "What's this?"

"Invitation to our author event." She pointed to the book in his bag. "The author of that series is coming tonight to sign books and answer questions. You should stop by."

"Maybe I will, thanks." He slipped the paper into his pocket and headed for the door. He took one step outside and rapidly jumped back inside. He pressed his back against the wall in between the door and the window.

Arya looked at him in surprise. "Something wrong?"

"Someone I'd rather not run into just made an appearance."

Arya looked out the window and he knew who she was looking at. A woman, about medium height and build, with long chestnut hair and tanned skin.

He had only caught a glimpse of her as she rounded the corner but her scent had preceded her and alerted him to the trouble. It gave him just enough time to duck.

Tiana.

He cursed under his breath.

How did she find me?

No one had known he was leaving town.

Undoubtedly she'd spotted his car. Now she was using scent to track him.

Damn, she's persistent.

Hopefully the sandalwood would mask his scent and throw her off the trail.

"You might want to hide. She's coming in."

"Crap," he hissed. He dove behind the counter and the stacked boxes of books behind it.

The bell chimed.

"Welcome, can I help you find something?"

There was silence.

He resisted every urge to peek and see just what she was doing.

He was a coward.

Not only was he having Arya take care of a problem that wasn't hers, but he was alpha. He shouldn't have a problem telling one of his pack to go home and leave him be. But, this was Tiana. He knew the minute she spotted him she would run back to the elders, fake tears at the ready, and have them drag him back home so he could be pestered about mating with her.

"You can come out now."

He looked up to see Arya peering over the boxes at him.

He stood up, brushed off his pants and said, "Sorry about that. Didn't mean to panic."

"I know it's none of my business, well, actually, it is a bit since it was my counter you hid behind." She quirked an eyebrow and grinned. "When a man has to dive for cover as if a grenade were going off, it's time for a restraining order."

He sighed, "If only it were that simple." He moved back around the counter. "Thanks again for the cover."

"No problem. It was strange. She came in, stared at me, and walked out."

Tiana had been scenting. But, luckily, with the sandalwood burning, she wouldn't smell him on Arya.

"Weird. Well, she shouldn't bother you since she didn't find me here. Thanks again."

He turned and walked out of the book shop. He went to his car, carefully looking and scenting for Tiana, climbed in and drove off. He parked a block away from Arya's house. The first thing he did was call his brother.

Ryker rumbled into the phone when he got the voicemail message. "Your ass is grass if I find out it was you who told Tiana where I was."

He clicked off the phone and decided to leave his phone and his wallet locked in his car. He slid the keys into his pocket and headed back to the house. He hopped the fence to the backyard, ducked behind a shrub and changed. He hid his clothes and climbed the steps of the porch to wait.

He knew it would be a few hours yet until Arya came home. Doing a few turns on the door mat, he made himself comfortable and allowed himself the luxury of a nap.

It was the sound of the front door opening that woke him. He hadn't heard her car pull up. He stretched and sat up to wait for the back door to open.

It didn't.

He sniffed the air.

Burnt cinnamon.

Only one person he knew of smelt like that and he'd only met the person once.

It wasn't Arya.

He darted off the deck and to the fence. He tried several times in vain to leap over but it was too high.

In desperation he started to frantically dig.

Dirt flew in all directions.

Just as he was able to stick his muzzle under the wooden gate he heard her car pull into the driveway.

His heart stopped.

No! He'll kill you.

He hysterically barked and howled to her.

She called from the other side of the house. "I'm coming, I'm coming."

Her keys jingled.

He didn't have time to think.

He ran back far enough to give himself momentum and charged at the gate.

It splintered on its hinges but didn't break.

He shook himself and backed away further.

She mounted the steps to the front door.

NO!

He raced at the gate again.

It crashed open under his weight and he was out like a shot.

Keys in the door.

Door opening.

A shot.

A scream.

A howl.

The Sapphire Named Ruby

Ruby spun herself in front of the mirror. Tall and slim, she looked lovely in her costume.

The halter top piece and skirt shimmered the deepest amethyst. The top piece was embroidered with sparkling gold thread that caught the light every time she moved. The skirt reached her ankles and split up both sides to expose her long legs while dancing. A kerchief piece with numerous gold-plated disks sewn into it wrapped around the waist of the skirt.

She sat back down at the vanity and touched up her lavender frost eye shimmer and the rest of her makeup.

Like most elf females, she had lovely angled eyes, a soft mouth, and sharp pointed ears that, tonight, were adorned with an amethyst earring. Her skin was on the dark side. She'd heard her complexion compared to fresh sugarcane or polished amber. She liked to think of her skin as fawn.

She grabbed the brush and made sure there wasn't a single tangle in her straight sapphire hair. It was getting long, reaching her waist now which was new for her. She ran the brush through it several times, smiling as the bristles glided through the thick, soft locks.

A knock came at the door.

She called, "Who is it?"

The stage director called, "Two minutes, Ruby."

"Thank you, Tobar."

Tonight they were fortunate to be in an indoor theater. Most places they had performed were outdoor amphitheaters which made the colder fall nights hard on the performers. She was grateful they headed south during the winter months which allowed them to perform all year. Otherwise they'd freeze to the stage floor.

One last turn before the mirror assured her that all was as it should be then she exited the dressing room. Her bare feet padded down the hall and behind the stage where other performers were readying themselves.

Her family hadn't believed it proper for her to want to be a performer. They allowed her to dance, but only appropriate dances with an acceptable instructor. Their station in life demanded that their daughter grow up to be a respectable elven lady; to grow up, marry a respectable male from another respectable family, have respectable children, and live a respectable life just like theirs. She, however, felt no joy in her life being decided for her.

Looking back, it was really their fault that she ran away.

Knowing her love of dance, they had allowed her to visit the traveling show when it had come to town.

For her family, it was the beginning of the end.

Her chaperone, an elderly goblin who had been her nanny all her life, was of poor eyesight and hearing. It was more like Ruby was chaperoning her than the other way around. But while the white-haired creature sat beside her and knit during the entire performance, Ruby was mesmerized.

The costumes glittered and glowed. The dancers flowed like water over the stage and the acrobats flew about despite their lack of wings. The music sang through her veins; the drum beats made her want to leap up and obey an older, more primal urge.

The end of the show came and the audience roared in delight.

She had remained in her seat, her mind whirling and her fingers itching.

She only had the one chance.

Outside the theater, she waited patiently for the coach. When it clattered to a stop in front of them she motioned for the driver to stay in his seat while she assisted her nanny inside. She herself then stepped up to get into the coach, making it rock slightly from her weight but she quickly stepped back down and shut the door loudly enough to be heard by the driver.

Thinking nothing wrong, the driver clicked the reins and the horses trotted down the street, leaving her behind.

"I was wondering if you'd stick around."

Ruby spun around, eyes wide, as she took in the harpy girl leaning against the wall; her auburn wings wrapped around herself to keep her warm and hide her body. Red hair was pulled high into a tail and her eyes were heavily done in blue charcoal.

The harpy smiled, revealing sharp teeth as she looked Ruby up and down. "Not bad," she mused. "You could do well here; with proper training you'll be doing spins in your sleep." She pushed off from the wall. "Follow me."

Ruby hesitated and glanced at where the coach had disappeared. It wasn't too late to go home and forget about the dreamy thoughts playing in her mind's eye.

The girl called, "I don't make offers twice." She slipped around the corner of the building.

Ruby bolted after her, lifting the skirt of her dress to keep from tripping.

They navigated down the alley between the theater and the building next to it and emerged into a large lot. What looked to be a normally empty space was filled with gypsy vardo-style caravans painted in a myriad of colors and designs. Some had windows on the sides and sported flower boxes spilling with colorful blooms. Others were enclosed but doors were open to let in the cool night air.

All manner of creatures were running about the camp site.

She saw goblins catching clothes and costumes that were being flung haphazardly from caravans. Performers were taking off their wigs and makeup as they walked to their homes. Some paused to chat with other parties as they passed by.

The smell of food being cooked wafted her way. How was it that simple carnival food smelt far better than the prepared meals she had at home? Her mouth watered.

The harpy girl passed it all by except to respond to a greeting or question being thrown her way. She only stopped in front of the largest caravan. Its entirety was painted black and decorated in strange golden symbols that ran from roof to base. Ruby could only distinguish the door from the rest of the structure when the harpy stepped up to it.

The girl knocked once and opened the door, motioning her in. "Madame Calypso will see you. But be warned, she doesn't take kindly to shy and scared creatures. Know what you want. If you hesitate or your mind is unsure she will reject you."

Did she know what she wanted; truly know?

Ruby nodded, drew herself up to her full height, shoulders back, and stepped in.

Ruby didn't remember much of what had happened or what the conversations had been. Madame Calypso remained shrouded in darkness. Ruby remembered the smell of incense, strong incense, strange cards, and the pricking of her finger.

A crash outside.

A scream.

Whatever hold that had been held over her broke as she leapt to her feet.

Outside, soldiers were tearing open doors and knocking tables over. The head of the guard, an elf, was looking about with unfeeling eyes.

"My father's guards!"

"Stay here, child," Madame Calypso purred.

Ruby winced as the darkness was suddenly illuminated by candles. The Madame came into full view.

A beautiful beaded dress draped over her svelte figure. Golden fur covered her body and her eyes were so green that emeralds would pale in comparison.

A sphynx!

Calypso passed by Ruby and, blocking her, stood leisurely in the doorway. "Can we help you, gentlemen?"

The Captain strode up when he heard them being addressed. At first, he was stunned silent by the creature before him.

Calypso smiled, revealing sharp canines. "My performers don't give… after hour performances. So if that's why you're all so aggressive, you'll have to go to the pleasure district."

Ruby had never seen the Captain blush before.

He coughed into his hand and tried to resume his cold demeanor. "The Lord's daughter has gone missing. She was last seen here. Her nanny returned home but our young Mistress was not with her."

"I'm afraid you're barking up the wrong tree, dear."

"You'll forgive me if I don't believe carnies."

She chuckled, "Not at all. We did see a young girl come through here wearing very fine clothes. She'd asked to join our troop but I had to turn her away. Couldn't risk my people's safety." Her eyes roamed over the current destruction being done. "I can see it was an effort wasted."

"We will continue our search regardless."

Her fur bristled, "Continue your search in a civilized manner or I will be forced to do something drastic. Your charge is not here and is probably home by now or lost down some vacant alley while you waste your time. I will see that your Lord pays compensation for the rash and reckless behavior of your men. I'm sure your Lord's reputation will love the scandal of his men barging in on naked female performers looking for a good time."

His face paled. He barked a single order and the men jumped to obey. They returned to his side in two ordered rows. He did an about face, his men mirrored, and they marched out of the lot.

The troupe was silent as they watched the men leave.

The moment the soldiers were out of sight the lot erupted into a cacophony of questions and complaints. Calypso held up a hand for silence.

It was instant.

She waited calmly, as if expecting something. When nothing further happened, she addressed the crowd. "Pack up everything. Leave nothing behind. Get the horses; we leave now."

Ruby's eyes widened at the sudden flurry of activity. Everyone jumped to obey Calypso's orders and none gave Ruby a second glance.

Calypso gently pushed Ruby out from behind her to the waiting harpy.

"Ruby has signed her contract. There is an empty caravan at the end of the lot that will be hers. Her training starts tomorrow."

****

That was six years ago.

"Good luck, Ruby."

"You look lovely. Do your best."

"Best performance yet, Ruby."

She pulled herself out of her memories and thanked everyone who wished her well.

This was her family, more of a family than her own had ever been to her. It was because of them, and their training, that she'd done so well.

She'd learned everything from how to work backstage on the sets and backdrops, to how to mend and sew costumes. When she'd proven herself, she was allowed to begin learning to perform. She'd demonstrated herself to be a determined young woman and worked tirelessly for anything she wanted. The people around her wanted her to succeed and, enthusiastically, encouraged and guided her.

Was there a process to gain their trust?

Yes.

Did they give her the worst possible jobs to start with?

Yes.

Scrubbing the stage with a brush, feeding and cleaning out animal cages, doing dishes every night after dinner, and even sitting out on cold nights to collect money for tickets.

It taught her to work hard; to grow a thick skin. It taught her that calluses weren't the end of the world and an aching when she crawled into bed meant she had done a good day's work.

Not only did Calypso take her on, she'd provided protection.

Five times over the years they'd run into her family's hired hands searching for Ruby to bring her home. The magic in the contract had shielded her from them. She didn't know the depths of the magic her employer possessed but it had demonstrated worthwhile at every obstacle.

But now... she wanted out.

As much as she loved to dance and adored the roar of an audience, there was something missing.

It was a hollowness that had snuck up on her. A gnawing, aching feeling that no amount of dancing or praise could seem to fill. Heavens knows she tried. Not even the affection of her friends could help.

Ruby had hoped for an easy parting of the ways when she had confessed to Calypso what she had been experiencing. Still she had not received an official answer and she feared she would be made to keep to her end of the contract.

No one but Calypso knew of her feelings and she couldn't break it to the others.

Not now.

She climbed the steps to the stage where a curtain shielded them from the audience's view.

Her partner was already on the stage.

Calypso herself had been Ruby's partner from the start of her performing career. Her golden fur was brushed and shined with health. Her hands and feet sported sharp claws on her fingers and toes. She wore a similar costume to Ruby's only green and her skirt was slightly modified to allow her tail freedom of movement. She was fixing a veil headpiece to her head, using hair pins to pin them to her ears.

Ruby nodded to Calypso.

Having learned to tune out the noise of the crowd on the other side of the curtain, she began to center herself for the show at hand.

She turned her back to Calypso and Calypso did the same to her. They arched back to back and held their arms aloft, one foot each resting on toes.

The drums began.

The crow went silent.

The candles dimmed until the few on the stage were left to illuminate the two dancers. The curtain lifted and the crowd released a deafening applause. When the cacophony slowed to a stop, the drums got faster.

A tambourine shook.

The two dancers pushed off of each other in an instant.

Spinning.

Pivoting.

Whirling.

They worked in perfect harmony with the ever increasing drum beats, twisting their hips so that with each practiced step the disks at their waists chimed together.

Sweat glistened on Ruby's bare skin. She didn't even have to think about what she was doing. Practice and innate talent let her feet do the thinking for her. A calm had descended on her body and it reflected in her smile. Her hair flared around her with every turn like a veil. Her hands moved in natural grace and her hips continued to let the beat guide their contorting.

When the drums reached the climax of their beating she knew they were near the end. She and Calypso backtracked and were back to back once more to their starting pose.

The drum beats ceased the instant the dancers did.

The crowd rose to their feet and cheered. The building near shook with the force of the applause.

Ruby smiled, her panting slowing.

Still the hollowness remained.

Calypso asked just loud enough to be heard by Ruby, "Are you sure you want to leave all of this?"

The two righted themselves and took their bows.

"I need to."

"Well, if you want out, you know what you must do."

Ruby looked to Calypso who was fingering one of her emerald earrings. She knew what Calypso meant. She would have to pay back every penny Calypso had invested into her; the jewels, the clothes, anything that she herself hadn't purchased with her cut of the night's profits.

But the money she had earned with the troop wouldn't even come close to paying back her debts. It wouldn't even make a dent. She could only imagine the money spent on costumes alone.

Her smile slid from her face as she gazed out at the crowd, still cheering them on. This was all she had known for years and now that she wanted to escape it, it seemed she couldn't.

"Of course," Calypso added, "If you can't pay off what you owe me, there is another way."

The candles went out and the theater went black.

The applause halted.

A male voice, so close that it made her jump, spoke from the darkness. "It's a deal?"

Calypso replied, "Yes."

A single candle flickered to life.

Ruby staggered away from the towering figure before her.

He was cloaked from head to toe in black. He had to be at least seven feet tall. At her height of five-eight, he was enormous. The cloak kept him completely hidden to her eyes. The hood that covered his head shrouded his face in utter darkness.

Calypso turned to Ruby, arms crossed over her chest. "Your contract has been bought out, Ruby. Since you couldn't pay for it, he has. You'll be leaving with him tonight."

Her mouth hung open in horror.

"W-what-"

"You wanted out, Ruby. You couldn't afford to buy out your contract so this was the only solution. Be happy I'm not forcing you to keep to our agreement."

She shook.

Her breath caught in her throat.

Her heart threatened to break free of her chest.

She turned to run but her feet stuck fast to the floor.

She looked down and screamed.

The floor was swallowing her whole.

She looked back to the stranger and saw by his posture that he was watching her. He had used magic to keep her from running. But how? She hadn't heard him move, hadn't heard him utter a word to indicate that he had done this. Was this Calypso's doing; ensuring that she didn't escape?

She scrambled to grab hold of anything to keep from sinking. Like quick sand, she sank lower and lower until she could no longer move her arms.

She tried desperately to keep her head up.

The magic dragged her under.

She became lost in the darkness.

About the Author

S.M. Nevermore has had a passion for all things paranormal from a young age. She lives in a small town in Massachusetts with her familiar, a very lazy orange cat, and her family. She is currently working on many other short stories and a larger novel that will become a trilogy.

https://www.facebook.com/S.M.Nevermore/

https://twitter.com/SMNevermore

Here are some of Nevermore's works:

Tales of the Paranormal
Short Stories of Curious Intrigue
S. M. NEVERMORE

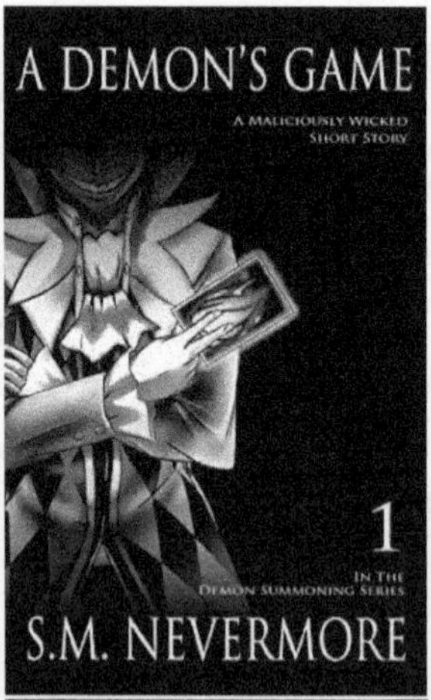
A DEMON'S GAME
A MALICIOUSLY WICKED SHORT STORY
1
IN THE DEMON SUMMONING SERIES
S.M. NEVERMORE

Masquerade
a romantically mysterious short story
S. M. Nevermore

The Yule Tree
S. M. NEVERMORE

HAUNTING AT SPIDER GATE CEMETERY
S. M. NEVERMORE

A Familiar's Guidance
S. M. NEVERMORE

SO, YOU FINALLY DIED!
A PARANORMAL SHORT STORY
S. M. NEVERMORE
BOOK 1: THE WAITING ROOM

CPSIA information can be obtained
at www.ICGtesting.com
Printed in the USA
BVHW030913021019
560008BV00001B/130/P